P9-BJM-050

OVERWATCH

REED MONTGOMERY BOOK 1

LOGAN RYLES

Copyright © 2019 by Logan Ryles. All rights reserved.

No part of this book may be reproduced in any form or by any electronic or mechanical means, including information storage and retrieval systems, without written permission from the publisher, except for the use of brief quotations in a book review.

OVERWATCH is a work of fiction. Names, characters, places, and incidents either are the product of the author's imagination or are used fictitiously. Any resemblance to actual persons, living or dead, events, or locales is entirely coincidental.

Paperback ISBN: 978-1-7323819-3-3

Hardcover ISBN: 978-1-7323819-5-7

Library of Congress Control Number: 2019904495

Published by Ryker Morgan Publishing.

Cover design by Rafido Designs.

ALSO BY LOGAN RYLES

The Reed Montgomery Series

Prequel: *Sandbox*, a short story (read for free at LoganRyles.com)

Book 1: *Overwatch*

Book 2: *Hunt to Kill*

Book 3: *Total War*

Book 4: *Smoke and Mirrors*

Book 5: *Survivor*

Book 6: *Death Cycle*

Book 7: *Sundown*

The Prosecution Force Series

Book 1: *Brink of War*

Book 2: *First Strike*

Book 3: *Election Day*

Book 4: *Failed State*

The Wolfgang Pierce Series

Prequel: *That Time in Appalachia* (read for free at

LoganRyles.com)

The Mason Sharpe Series

For my darling Anna

Everything I ever wrote I wrote for you.

1

Cape May
New Jersey

Jersey was cold. The first breath of impending winter blew down off the North Atlantic, whistling softly between the pilings and over the coarse sand of Cape May's south beach. Reed stood at the waterline, feeling every icy breath of wind as it whipped around the collar of his wetsuit, but he didn't shiver. He stood perfectly still, and with a pair of binoculars, he surveyed the mouth of the Delaware Bay.

Two-foot waves glimmered under the blaze of a full moon, and the water lapped against the barnacle-covered feet of pier pilings, washing back and forth across the rocky sand shore. Thirty miles to the northeast, the neon lights of Atlantic City glimmered on the horizon. In the opposite direction, the dark outline of Cape Henlopen State Park was barely visible, marked by half a dozen twinkling campfires. Red and green

buoys guarded the entrance to the bay, and an occasional fish jumped into the moonlight, shining between
the waves.

But it was the emptiness that hallmarked the night.
The isolation. Ideal conditions for a kill.

Reed lowered the binoculars and breathed in the
cold air. It stung his lungs like the prick of a million
needles, but the salt breeze tasted fresh. He squinted
toward the horizon, then raised the binoculars again
and swept his gaze across the bay twice more. On the
third pass, he paused over an irregularity in the water
—a rolling wave that moved against the current, away
from shore. Turning back to the left, he found the
source of the disturbance—a thirty-foot yacht, running
dark, without a hint of humanity on board.

He studied the boat, then crouched in the sand,
depositing his binoculars into a backpack and with-
drawing a small case. After snapping it open, he withdrew a Glock 26 subcompact pistol, loaded the weapon
with a single magazine containing ten rounds of frag-
menting hollow points, and racked the slide. Salt spray
gleamed on the gun under the light of the moon. Every
curve and edge of the weapon felt hard and cold, but
familiar, like a favorite pair of shoes or a worn baseball
cap.

With the gun tucked into the interior of his wetsuit,
Reed pulled a pair of diver's goggles over his face, and
the air rushed from his lungs the moment he stepped
into the chilled water. One breath, then another, both
slow and measured against the chills that ripped up his
spine. Then he waded out until the sandy bottom

slipped from under his fins. The Jersey shoreline faded behind him as he cut through the waves, drawing occasional breaths between wide breaststrokes.

Fifteen minutes of powerful kicking brought Reed four hundred yards offshore, where he stopped to tread water and reposition on the yacht. As he anticipated, it now sat at anchor outside the mouth of the bay, bobbing in the rolling waves. The boat remained dark and silent, but Reed wasn't perturbed. He floated upright in the water, treading between deep breaths as he continued to regulate his breathing. His heart thumped, but he didn't feel as cold anymore. The water trapped between the wetsuit and his skin had warmed from the vigorous exercise and now served to insulate him from the frigid water. Five minutes passed before he detected the first sign of life on board the vessel. It came in the form of a muffled shout, followed by a dull thud.

One deep breath of damp air, then Reed dove into the black water. Kicking out with both legs, he approached the boat underwater, clearing the last fifty yards in under two minutes. When he surfaced, he bobbed feet from the yacht's wide swim deck. He hoisted himself up and landed on the platform without a sound. Water drained off the wetsuit and back into the ocean as he sat, listening for any noise from inside the boat. Voices were barely audible, stifled by the thick fiberglass and teak trim of the expensive pleasure cruiser. Somewhere inside the cabin were at least two men. Both American. Both with northeastern accents.

On the platform, he twisted and then unlatched his

fins, depositing them and the mask onto the swim deck. He turned and flipped over the bulkhead, his bare feet landing on the deck without a sound.

The rear of the boat consisted of a row of luxury lounge chairs followed by a narrow stairwell to the cockpit and a door to the main salon. A visual sweep of the rear of the cockpit confirmed that all occupants of the boat were inside the salon.

He unzipped his wetsuit and withdrew the Glock, subconsciously performing a press check on the chamber. The glimmer of the brass casing in the dull moonlight assured him that the weapon was hot, and he proceeded to the door of the cabin. His heart continued to thump as a rush of adrenaline charged his blood with invisible lightning. His hands didn't shake, but that was due to years of practice containing the anxiety and anticipation of an impending kill.

This is it.

The latch lifted without resistance, and the door swung inward. Lights shone from somewhere beyond the hallway. Something heavy scraped against the hardwood flooring, and the air reeked of cigarette smoke.

Stepping across the threshold, Reed raised his weapon and then rounded the corner into the lounge, where two men sat at a card table. One man was dark and slim and wore an expensive evening suit and designer eyeglasses. He sat against the far wall, leaning over the table and growling at his companion between clenched teeth.

The second man was short and broad, stuffed into a

polo shirt that constricted around each layer of fat, making him look like a caterpillar fighting to break free of an undersized cocoon. He puffed on a cigarette as sweat streamed down his bold, Italian-American features.

Both men looked up when the stranger burst into the lounge. The short man with the cigarette choked and pushed himself away from the table, crashing to the floor and gurgling something unintelligible. The man in the suit glared up at the intruder with wide, panicked eyes and reached under his coat.

Reed didn't hesitate. The Glock barked twice, spitting 9mm slugs across the salon at over twelve hundred feet per second, and scarlet oozed from the folds of the man's suit. He fell limp against the wall, his hand still caught beneath the jacket, and his mouth flopped open, a trail of blood running down his chin.

The man on the floor screamed and wriggled his way backward, holding one hand out toward Reed.

"Hey! What do you want? Just chill, all right? I've got nothin' to do wid him!"

The boat swayed over another wave as Reed stepped across the salon and trained the pistol on the chubby man. Every part of Reed's body was alive with tension, now. He could feel it in his bones. In the thunder of blood rushing through his brain. In the weight of the gun clenched between his fingers.

But instead of pulling the trigger, he spoke in a calm, monotone voice.

"Where's the money?"

The chubby man frowned, swallowed, and blinked

all at once. "What? The money? Look, man. I don't know nothin' about no money! I'm just his valet, okay? I don't even know why I'm here!"

Reed squatted on the floor and leaned toward his cornered prey. He reached between the man's legs and gripped the crotch of his khakis. Without a sound, Reed tightened his hold around the wadded pants, digging his fingers into the folds of the cloth while keeping the pistol trained on the man's face.

The man's eyes grew wide, and his gut jiggled as he restrained a scream. Tears streamed down his face.

"Man, please . . . let me go!"

Reed pressed the barrel of the gun against his victim's left eye socket and laid his finger against the trigger. At the same moment, he clenched with his left hand and twisted.

"Last chance. Where's the money?"

The chubby man screamed and fell against the wall, choking on his saliva as he attempted to pull away from the gun.

"All right! All right! It's in the trunk of a taxi. New York. Medallion 7J59."

Something in his eyes—maybe it was the fear, or the shadow of truth passing through those wide windows and into his terrified soul—whatever it was, Reed believed him. He released his hold around the pants and took half a step back.

The chubby man gasped and covered his crotch with both hands, sobbing as he leaned against the mahogany paneling. "I swear, it's the truth. It's all there!"

Reed walked across the cabin to an emergency locker mounted midway up the wall. From an orange case, he withdrew a twelve-gauge flare gun and loaded a single waterproof cartridge into the chamber. He tucked the gun into his wetsuit, then zipped it back up.

"I believe you," Reed said. "It's your lucky day."

The man on the floor panted, his face still flooded with pain as he shielded his crotch.

"I swear to God, man. I wouldn't lie."

Why do the double-dipping swindlers always wait until their backs are against the wall before they tell the truth?

Reed walked to one of the salon's big bay windows, pushed it open, and sucked in a breath of fresh air. A quick visual inspection confirmed that they were still alone in the mouth of the bay, and Reed turned toward the liquor cabinet. He withdrew a pint of Kentucky bourbon, twisted the cap off, and handed it to the man on the floor.

"Drink."

"Huh?" Confusion flooded his wide eyes.

Reed pushed the pint into his hand and then raised the Glock again. "Drink," he repeated.

The man on the floor raised the bottle and took a swig of the harsh liquor. He choked and tried to lower the bourbon, but he was stopped by the pressure of the Glock jammed into his rib cage.

"Keep going. All of it."

He spluttered and gulped the alcohol in unbridled panic as more of it streamed down his chin and over his shirt. Every time he tried to lower the bottle, Reed shoved the gun deeper into his skin, twisting and biting into him through his dirty polo shirt.

At last, the bottle was empty, and it clattered to the floor amid a puddle of whiskey. The chubby man coughed and leaned back, wheezing and struggling to catch his breath as saliva dripped from his lips.

"Dammit, man. I swear I'm telling the truth."

Too little too late—like Judas apologizing to a bloody cross. Reed cocked his left fist and drove a snapping punch to the backside of the man's skull. His victim slumped over in instant unconsciousness.

Reed picked up a towel from the galley counter, wiped down the grip of the Glock, and then placed it in the hand of the man on the floor, pushing the chubby finger through the trigger guard. He stood and surveyed the scene, double-checking each step to ensure he hadn't missed something. Everything looked good, and Reed retreated to the rear deck and surveyed the horizon for any sign of other boats. As before, the bay was dark and empty.

After affixing the fins back onto his feet and pulling the mask over his face, he slipped into the cold water and kicked toward shore. When he was fifty yards away from the yacht, he drew the waterlogged flare gun from his wetsuit and aligned the sights with the main salon. He squeezed the plastic trigger. The gun popped, and the flare shot across the water, arcing perfectly through the open window and crashing into the lounge. A moment later, smoke and flames rose from the window as the flare ignited the puddle of whiskey inside.

Reed watched the scene, imagining that he could feel the heat of the fire on his icy face.

A few powerful kicks propelled his muscular frame through the water and back toward shore. He dropped the flare gun, allowing it to fade into the darkness as he closed his eyes. He pictured the flames of the yacht and imagined it sinking, slipping between the waves and carrying the bodies to the bottom of the bay and the watery grave it promised.

Twenty-nine.

2

North Georgia

The foothills and ravines rose and fell much like the waves of the night before, rising until they almost touched the morning sun, then falling again into a shadow-filled valley, carrying the road with them. Orange and brown leaves drifted down from overhanging hardwoods, bouncing across the pavement before being washed into the ditch. The last remnants of a dying summer. Everything felt crisp and clean.

The stillness of the mountain road was shattered by the roar of the black car, low-slung, with tinted windows and exhaust that shook the mountains to their roots. It blasted around a hillcrest and hurtled into a valley, every curve of the road shoving the car toward the edge, sending wide tires screaming over scarred asphalt, threatening to break free and roll into a ditch at any moment. After another bark of exhaust and a thunderous roar of the oversized engine, the car pulled out of the turn and rocketed forward again.

Reed didn't know the road. He'd never traveled that way before. Each turn was unknown, filled with hidden danger and intoxicating peril. He slammed the Camaro into fourth gear and dumped the clutch. The leather-wrapped steering wheel was damp in his hands, slipping between his fingers as he allowed the car to self-correct out of another turn. Wind ripped through the open windows, flooding the car with the mixed scents of autumn flowers and burning gasoline. It was the kind of smell dreams were made of.

Downshift back to third. Ride the brake and turn to the left. Pull out, half-throttle, just in time to break a slide and prevent the car from spinning into a ravine. The mountains clapped and shook as the exhaust backfired, a sound like a gunshot ripping through the trees. Reed sucked in a lungful of crisp air and relaxed off the throttle, allowing the car to glide to a natural halt at a stop sign. He closed his eyes and listened to the rumble of the V-8. The way the exhaust snarled, even at idle. It was like music, but better than any orchestra the world had ever heard. It was a voice that awoke the deepest parts of his soul, whispering to his heart sweeter than any lover ever could.

Freedom captured in an engine block.

Reed leaned back in the tight racing seat and slid on his sunglasses, then turned to the left and merged onto a four-lane highway. A green sign towered next to the roadway, painted with reflective letters:

ATLANTA, 127 MILES

The roar of the motor receded to a muted rumble as Reed rolled up the windows and ran one hand through his close-cropped hair. The four-lane road brought its own unique thrill: the peace of an American muscle car cruising an American highway. Another taste of freedom tainted by the irrefutable truth that it was only that—a taste.

The icy water and dancing flames of the night before receded into the back of his mind, but they would never fade away completely. They joined a slideshow of twenty-eight other bloody moments over the past three years—moments when Reed stepped into somebody's life and snuffed it out. Every night, that slideshow was the last thing he saw before drifting into oblivion. Every morning it was the first thing that flooded his mind, even before consciousness returned. He couldn't tell the difference between regret or repulsion—whether he felt guilt or simple trauma at the memories. Maybe it was all the same thing. Maybe it didn't matter. The only thing that really mattered was the other side of the list, a number that shrank each time he completed a job. A number that promised freedom when it dropped to zero.

A dull buzz rang from the console, jarring Reed from his thoughts. He hit the accept button on the dash, and the call switched to the speaker system.

"It's done," he said.

The voice that answered sounded sleepy, or maybe

drunk. With Brent, there was no way to tell. It could've been both.

"Sweet, dude. I saw the news. It looks like you implemented a little arson. Good stuff."

"Did they salvage the boat?"

"Nah, man, it sank. A few locals took pictures, but there's nothing to worry about. Looks like you cleaned up real nice." The blend of spunk and dismissal in Brent's voice was the sort of casual enthusiasm only a stoned cheerleader could master. Or, in this case, a hitman's handler.

"Good. They won't find much when they raise it."

"Well, it's sitting in fifty feet of water, so it'll take time. They'll probably lift the bodies today."

"Won't be much left," Reed said. "He's got enough alcohol in his stomach to knock out a linebacker."

"Right, right. And the goods?"

"The money is in the trunk of a taxi. New York City. I emailed you the medallion number."

"You checked it out?"

"No, but it's there."

"Sure, man. Whatever you say."

Reed adjusted the phone against his ear and shifted into overdrive. The tachometer dropped, and the rumble of the motor faded into a hum. He heard Brent slurping on something. A drink, or maybe some hard candy.

"I'm ready for the next job," he said. "How soon can you line it up?"

"Um . . . dude, you haven't been paid for the last

one." Brent smacked his lips. "Don't you wanna catch
your breath?"

"I prefer to stay busy. What do you have?"

"I hadn't planned on booking you. I've only got one
gig right now, and I didn't think you'd want it. It's a
Georgia State Senator. Atlanta hit."

"That's perfect. Book me."

Brent chomped down with an explosion of wet
crunching. Yes, definitely hard candy. "You sure, man? I
mean, that's practically your backyard. You shouldn't
shit where you eat."

"I'm not worried about it. Just book the hit and send
me the file."

"Don't you wanna know what it pays?"

"Nope." Reed hit the end-call button, then dropped
the shifter out of overdrive and planted his foot into the
accelerator.

Atlanta: 116 miles.

"Don't twist it so hard. You'll strip it." The big greasy
hand fell over Reed's, guiding him around one quarter
turn of the wrench. "There. Just like that. Twist till it
stops, then a quarter turn. No more."

Reed lay on the concrete and gazed up at the underside of the engine block, painted bright red with streaks
of oil and grease crisscrossing it at random. His percep-
tions were clouded by a misted, dreamlike state,
making everything he touched and each word he heard
muted and distant. The big front tires hung six inches

off the ground, just high enough for him to slip his little arm under. He imagined the car falling off the jack stands and jerked his arm back as a wave of thrill surged through his narrow chest.

"Hand me that socket wrench."

Reed felt the cool metal of the wrench between his greasy fingers. It was heavy and difficult to lift in the awkward position beneath the car. His hand looked tiny as he passed the wrench to the man lying beside him. Dave Montgomery took the wrench and slipped it over a sway bar link, twisted until it stopped, then gave it a quarter turn more.

"Will it be faster, Dad?" Reed asked.

Dave fiddled with the linkage, running a clean rag over the bar and toward the wheel hub.

"Speed is nothing if you can't control it, Reed. Tighter sway bars are all about control. Feeling the road when you turn. Keeping the tires planted on the pavement. You understand what I'm saying?"

Reed nodded. He watched in transfixed fascination as Dave lifted a grease gun and lubricated the joints of the front suspension. Grease dripped off the car and splattered on the garage floor.

Dave grabbed a rag and wiped up the spill.

"A good mechanic wouldn't spill grease. That means you've used too much. These tiny brass fittings here? You can tell a lot about a man by what he calls them. An ignoramus might call them a nipple. But a real motorhead knows they're called a zerk."

Reed giggled. "A zurt?"

"No, a zerk."

"That's a funny word."

Dave smiled as he picked up the grease gun again and began to crawl from beneath the car. Reed followed him, scraping his bare knees against the dirt. Dave held out his hand and helped Reed to his feet, then handed him the rag.

"Wipe off your hands. Time to give her a whirl."

The rough rag ground into his little palms as he scrubbed the grease away. Streaks of brown tarnished the red cloth, leaving his palms red. The green car with silver rally wheels sat with its front end lifted on jack stands, the hood raised to expose the big motor. Twin white rally stripes ran over the hood and the deck of the trunk. A chrome badge, glued to the fender just behind the front wheel, read "Camaro" in graceful italics. Beyond it, just in front of the wheel, another chrome badge was accented with red trim: *Z/28.*

Reed touched the emblem, running his finger down the Z and beneath the numbers. His skin left a thin sheen of oil, reflecting in the dull light of the setting sun. He smiled, then looked up at his dad.

"Will we wash it today?"

Dave laughed. "Boy, you love to wash a car. No, we don't have time today, but let's turn it over and see how she sounds. Here. Hop in."

A silver key ring flashed in the air. Reed caught it with both hands, and his knees felt suddenly stiff as his fingers closed around the key. He stared down at the glistening silver, blank except for the etched Chevrolet bow tie. "Are you serious?" he mumbled.

"Of course I'm serious. Get in."

Reed didn't wait for him to change his mind. He opened the heavy door and piled onto the worn vinyl seat. It was warm from the blaze of the Alabama sun beating down through the garage door, but it felt like home. He scooted to the front of the seat and strained his left leg to reach for the clutch. His shoe slipped off the edge of the pedal, and he slid closer to the wood-lined steering wheel.

"Okay. First the clutch, all the way to the floor. Then turn it over."

The key clicked against the tumblers as Reed slipped it into the ignition. He bit his lip and pressed the clutch to the floor. It was heavy, and he had to brace himself on the edge of the seat to force the pedal against the floorboard. Then he twisted the key. The starter whined, and the car jolted as the big motor turned over. Once. Twice.

"Give it a little gas, son. Just tap the pedal."

Reed laid his right foot against the pedal and tapped the gas. The car coughed and lurched again, turning over twice more. The exhaust rumbled, and the motor roared to life, sending shockwaves ripping down the body of the car. Reed felt it in the steering wheel. He felt it in the pedals and through the seats. The Camaro shook and thundered; it was an awakened monster, alive and hungry.

"Dad! It's working. It's running!" Reed laughed and ran his hands over the steering wheel. He felt every dimple in the wood and the sharp edge of the metal spokes. He watched the tachometer dance and spike as the engine continued to cough on a bad tune. But it sounded so good. The feeling flooded his body, filling him with warmth and power.

"That's my boy!" Dave leaned through the window and grinned down at Reed. He patted him on the back, then gave his shoulder a squeeze. "You're a natural. The car trusts you. I can hear it."

Reed closed his eyes and bit his lip. His tongue poked between the gap in his teeth. The vibrations rumbled up his spine and pounded in his head. Nothing had ever felt so good.

"Can I help you?" Dave shouted over the roar of the car.

In the distance, Reed heard tires grind against concrete. Something shone across his eyes, and he snapped them open. Red and blue lights flashed in the rearview mirror, and he craned his neck to look behind him. Two black cars were stopped halfway down the long driveway, and tall men in dark suits and sunglasses piled out. They walked toward his father, and one of them flashed a gold badge. Stern wrinkles lined their jaws and foreheads, as though their faces were carved in stone.

"David Montgomery?"

"Yes . . . what can I do for you?"

"Turn around and place your hands behind your back, please."

A cold fist closed inside of Reed's stomach. The smile faded from his lips as he stared through the back glass. The men shoved his father over the rear of the Camaro and planted his face against the decklid of the trunk. His cheeks flushed red, while his eyes widened with strain. He spluttered and tried to lift his head, but the bigger man forced him down again.

"David Montgomery, you are under arrest. The charge is four counts of securities fraud, two counts of intentional deception of a federal agent, and eight counts of money laundering. You have the right to remain silent. Anything you say..."

The voices faded into a muted blur. Reed's stomach lurched toward his throat as big tears welled, stinging and burning like fire. He jerked the door handle and sprang from the car toward the bumper. The big men hauled Dave up by the elbows and propelled him toward the sedans.

"No! Dad, no!" Reed screamed, grabbed the nearest officer by the leg, and tried to shove him away. The big man leered down at him, grabbing him by the collar and flinging him onto the concrete.

"Get out of the way, kid. We'll get to you soon enough."

They faded away toward the cars. Reed ran after them, tears still streaming down his cheeks as he pounded the pavement. But the farther he ran, the farther away they seemed, lost in the swirl of mist. Another man, tall and menacing, appeared from behind a trash can. Dressed in muted green with a giant hard-brimmed hat, he backhanded Reed across the face, hurling him to the ground.

"Where the hell do you think you're going, recruit? You better fall in before I wipe my boot across your face! You haven't got the *guts* to be a Marine!"

Reed screamed and tried to crawl away. Darkness

closed around him, and metal bars sprung out of the ground, blocking his way, pressing in on every side and forcing him into a corner. Still screaming, he beat against the bars and kicked with both feet, but nobody answered. The darkness was so complete, he couldn't see his hands.

Then he heard a smooth, British voice just behind him. Reed whirled around to see a bald man with large ears, a broad, toothy smile, and deep grey eyes leaning toward him.

"Need a hand, son?" The man leaned down and offered his hand. "You're mine now."

Reed lurched out of bed, snatching a loaded SIG Sauer from the nightstand beside him and jamming it toward the leering face. He gasped for air and swung the pistol around the room, searching for a target, but none of the men were there. Not the cops, not the Marine drill sergeant, not the tall British man with big ears. They had all faded into the nightmare like every one before it.

Reed dropped the gun on the covers, pressed his face into his hands, and gasped for air again. His skin prickled, and a shiver racked his torso, chilling him under the breeze of the ceiling fan. He swung his feet out of the bed and stumbled across the loft and down the steps.

The interior of the cabin was still, and he gazed outside over the darkened forest. A night-light glowed against one wall, casting shadows across the hardwood floor. Baxter lay curled up in his favorite armchair, snoring like a dragon with sleep apnea. Drool ran out of the English bulldog's flopping lips, dripping onto the floor in a slow waterfall.

Reed stumbled to the refrigerator and retrieved a beer. He popped the cap off against the edge of the counter, and Baxter's ears pricked up. The old dog poked his head over the arm of the chair, snorting and lapping saliva off his lips, then stared at Reed with more than a hint of annoyance.

"Sorry, boy," Reed muttered. "You know how it is. Night thirst."

Baxter snorted again, then hopped down from the chair and trotted to his water bowl. He lapped up a couple swallows of water, then flopped down under the kitchen table and commenced to snoring again.

Reed watched him for a moment, smiling. Nothing kept Baxter awake. He could have slept through a tornado. The smile faded from Reed's lips as the emotional fallout of the dream sank over him. He gulped down more beer, trying to picture his father's warm smile, trying to recall the gentle laugh. As clear and strong as both had been only moments before, they now felt as old and distant as they truly were.

Almost every night for years, this same dream plagued his tired mind. At first, it was just the nightmare of his father being arrested, occasionally joined by haunted memories of the trial and conviction. After Reed joined the Marine Corps, the nightmare was expanded to include the drill sergeant—the big man with the big hat. Another shouting terror that had nothing to do with his childhood, and yet it dominated the dream as much as Dave Montgomery's violent arrest.

And then the bald man with big ears. So kind and gentle. So menacing. The kingpin killer.

Reed stumbled back up the stairs into the loft. He flipped the nightstand lamp on, then knelt beside the twin bed and reached beneath the overhanging sheets. His fingers closed around the hard edge of a box, wooden and cold, and he dragged it out then sat cross-legged on the floor. Reed took another long pull of beer, flipped the latch open, and lifted the lid.

Mementos lay inside: a few sheets of paper, five fake passports, a spare handgun, and fifty thousand dollars in cash. Reed shuffled the items aside and dug under the stack of papers. He felt the faded photograph under his fingers, recognizing it by its tattered edge, and pulled it free of the pile.

Under the soft glow of the lamp, he saw the green car sitting at the edge of a lake and shining under the sun. The chrome badges affixed to the fender glistened, half-covered by the family that sat in a neat line beside the car. A smiling Dave Montgomery on the right leaned next to his wife with one arm wrapped around her shoulders. Reed sat on his lap, barely six years old, his legs crossed much the same as they were now. The three of them radiated in that picture in a way that no amount of sunlight could fabricate. It was calm and perfect, the way they huddled together in front of that old '69 Z/28. A family together. Safe.

Reed blinked back the stinging in his eyes and shoved the photo into the pile of papers. He tipped the beer bottle up and gulped down the last few pulls of fizzy alcohol. Back in the box, he retrieved a small notebook about three inches tall with a rubber band holding it closed. He pulled the band off and flipped it open. His tight handwriting covered the first page in condensed notes.

March 17. Nova Scotia, Canada. Paul John Grier, age 37. Terminated by asphyxiation with vehicle exhaust. Body left for the police. One down, twenty-nine remaining. I feel as though I died with him.

He flipped a few more pages and then stopped at another entry, this one dated June seventh of the following year.

Marie Florence Thomas. Age 49. Panama City, Panama. Terminated by precision shot, five hundred yards. Body fell into canal. Confirmation of death obtained by secondary contractor. Twelve down, eighteen to go. This was the first woman.

Reed lifted a pencil from the box and flipped to the first blank page. He took a deep breath then scratched a new entry onto the yellow paper. His fingers trembled, and he bore down against the pencil until it bit into the paper.

October 29th. Max Chester. Middle name unknown. Delaware Bay, United States. Terminated by use of alcohol, fire, and drowning. Also had to terminate unknown man there with him. Both bodies lost to sea. Twenty-nine down, one to go. I'm almost free.

Reed stared at the note, rereading it once, then he shut the book, wrapped the rubber band back around it, and pushed the box beneath the bed. His phone dinged from the bedside, and he scooped it up. A notification lit the screen beside Brent's name. He unlocked the phone and opened the message.

HIT CONFIRMED. DETAILS TO FOLLOW.

3

Atlanta, Georgia

The lights of the nightclub were almost blinding. Reed sat at the bar, leaned over the counter, and stared into the muddled depths of a Jack and Coke. The ice melted slowly, and the surface of the drink pulsated with each pounding thump of the music.

Reed tipped the glass back, draining the contents, then slammed it back on the counter and nodded at the bartender.

"Make it a double."

A spunky young woman with a heavy Boston accent replaced his glass and poured three fingers from a bottle of Jack.

"Got a new Kentucky bourbon on special tonight. Wanna mix it up?"

Reed shook his head. "Last one, Jen. Gonna call it a night."

"You should stick around. We're playing live music later."

His phone vibrated in his pocket, and he pulled it out. The screen glowed, illuminating a text message from a contact labeled "O.E."

CALL ME.

Reed hesitated over the text, twisting the glass between his fingers and listening to the ice cubes tumble over one another. He dreaded this moment and the conversation it promised. For twenty-nine kills, his boss had maintained close tabs on Reed, checking in with him every few weeks and offering advice and training. Even knocking him over the head now and again, ensuring he was performing at the top of his game, every time. It was a strange relationship the two of them formed. Oliver Enfield was both master and friend, slaver and mentor. As the bodies piled up and Reed worked his way down the hit list, Oliver allowed him increased independence and allocated him larger paychecks.

For three years I served the U.S. Government, and I never felt as respected as I do by a total, black-hearted killer.

Reed mashed the call button and held the phone against his ear.

Oliver answered with just the hint of an English accent, abrupt but kind. "Reed. We should talk."

Reed lowered his head, covering his left ear.

"Oliver. It's not a great time. Can I call you back?"

"It's important. I want to talk to . . . about . . . kill . . ."

"I can't hear you. Oliver . . . you're breaking up."

The voice faded and crackled on the other end of

the line. Reed squinted at the phone and saw one bar illuminated in the top corner of the screen. It must be the nightclub. A metal roof or something.

"Oliver, I'm gonna call you back in ten, okay? I can't hear you."

As the music stopped and the flashing lights faded, Reed drained his glass, dropped a fifty on the counter, and nodded at the bartender.

"I'll catch you later."

He pressed his way into the crowd, glancing toward the corner stage as he heard the manager rambling into the microphone.

"A sensation. A Madonna of our time. Ladies and gentlemen, please welcome the incredible Sirena Wilder!"

The manager stepped back and clapped, and the room erupted in a gentle rumble of applause. The lights focused on the stage as the manager melted into the shadows, and just as Reed started to turn back toward the door, he saw her. The club fell silent, and the girl stood in front of the mic.

Reed stopped, curiosity overcoming his better judgment. He stared over the bobbing heads as the girl picked up a guitar and settled back on a stool. She brushed long blonde bangs from her view and ran her fingers across the strings. The club was breathlessly silent as the gentle melody of the guitar rippled through the audio system. Her face shone softly in the lights, and she stared at her fingers, strumming gently and rocking back and forth on the stool.

When she smiled at the crowd, Reed's heart

skipped. She had narrow, graceful features, and her high cheekbones highlighted rosy dimples. Her bright smile shone from her crystal-blue eyes, which were deep and soft, as though nothing ugly or sad had ever touched her life. She was tall and curvy, with just a hint of pudge, and she wore a spaghetti-strap top and jeans with torn-out knees. Her feet, encased in yellow converse sneakers, were tucked under the stool. Her hair fell in gentle waves over her bare shoulders, shining in the stage lights, showing just a touch of red amid the blonde.

Pressing back through the crowd, Reed sat down at the bar without taking his eyes off the stage. He rapped on the counter with his knuckles, and the bartender chuckled and slid him another whiskey.

The guitar intensified over the speakers, and the girl swayed and smiled, alight with passion and excitement. Slowly, she leaned forward and whispered into the mic.

"How we doing tonight, guys?"

The crowd cheered and clapped. Her voice was soft but clear, ringing with confidence, fun, and hint of a Southern accent. Reed swallowed his whiskey. Sirena leaned back on the stool and finger-picked a few more chords, flooding the small room with a crescendo of melody. She grinned, then leaned forward and abruptly stopped playing. With her lips millimeters from the mic, she began to sing softly.

"He was a vagrant and I a gypsy. I lost my way when he first kissed me."

Reed sat, motionless. Her voice was unlike anything

he had ever heard. It was soft, strong, and full of charm. She picked the guitar again, her voice rising with each chord change. When she hit the chorus she slapped the guitar with the palm of her hand between every strum, creating a perfect blend of rhythm and melody. She stood up from the stool and leaned toward the mic as she broke into the bridge. The crowd sang with her, swaying back and forth under the dim lights.

The song ended, and the bartender spoke over the applause. "She's from Decatur. Been playing here for a couple weeks and sings at a few bars around town. Getting kind of popular."

Reed slid his glass back down the counter for a refill, still watching the girl as she began her next song. The crowd talked amongst themselves, ordering drinks, and relaxing to the music. The girl played for another half hour, occasionally swapping the guitar for a keyboard. Her vocal talent ranged from pop to country to eighties rock-and-roll, and every song brought a new round of applause from the half-drunk audience. Still leaning against the bar at the back of the crowd, Reed joined in the show of appreciation.

When Sirena finished her final song, she waved to the audience and blew a kiss, then left through a door backstage. Reed stood and dropped another fifty on the counter. He almost started toward the stage, but the thumping club music and flashing strobe lights returned. He blinked in the blaze and shook his head.

I'm drunk. It's time to go home.

As he pushed through the crowd, he saw her again. She stood at the far end of the bar, leaning on the counter and laughing at a pair of gushing drunks. She offered them each a hug and then signed their cocktail napkins before they grinned and bumbled off. Sirena turned toward the bar, shouting something at the bartender over the blare of the music.

Reed shoved a couple drunks out of the way until he made his way to her. Sirena shuffled through her purse, peeling out a wad of one dollar bills and a handful of change. The bartender walked toward them with a cream-colored daiquiri and a fresh napkin.

Reed sat down on the stool beside her and reached into his pocket.

"May I?"

The girl squinted through the lights at his broad frame. Reed shifted on the stool, leaning down, trying to make himself look less like a killer.

She smiled. "Oh, you're sweet. But us Southern girls can buy our own drinks."

Her accent was evident now. Alabama, for sure. Or maybe Mississippi. The South never sounded so good.

Reed shook his head. "No. I insist. It was a great show."

He pulled a twenty from his wallet and passed it to the bartender. "Another, please."

Jen lifted one eyebrow. "A daiquiri?"

"Yeah . . . sure." Reed leaned on the counter and stared at Sirena as she took a deep sip of the drink then winked at him. The gesture was unexpected, and maybe it was meant to be sly, but it just looked cute.

"Where you from, cowboy?"

Reed cleared his throat. "Here and there."

"The city?"

"Sometimes. And you?"

Sirena took another long sip of the drink. "Mississippi. A little town you wouldn't have heard of."

Mississippi.

He knew it. Man, he loved Mississippi.

"Rebels fan?"

Sirena grinned. "Hell yeah! Damn right."

Reed felt the cold touch of glass in his hand and took a sip of the tangy drink. It was sweeter than he expected. "So what brings a Mississippi Rebel to the big city?"

"Fortune and fame. What else?"

She set the glass down and pulled a tube of lipstick from her purse. With practiced ease, she applied it to her lips then rubbed them together. Each motion was graceful, and confident. He liked it.

Sirena dropped the lipstick back into the purse, then laid a ten-dollar bill on the counter. "Thanks, Jen. I'll see you next week."

Reed pushed the bill back toward her. "I've got the drink. Wanna stay for another?"

Sirena laughed and winked at him. "Oh no, cowboy. I know how that game is played. This girl buys her own drinks. Thanks anyway. You're a champ." She smacked him on the arm and then stepped into the crowd.

A girl who buys her own drinks. Now that's something.

Reed stood up. "Wait. I like you."

Sirena stopped. Reed froze. What the hell did he just say? His throat was suddenly dry, and he cursed under his breath.

Idiot.

Sirena turned around, and a smirk played at the corners of her mouth. He thought she might jack slap him, but instead, she broke into a soft laugh. "Well, okay, then. Straight to the point. You ain't from around here."

His muscles relaxed, and he attempted a coy smile. "Isn't the mystery irresistible?"

She laughed again. "More desperate, I'm afraid. But there's a hint of charm . . . "

Sirena trailed off, but held his gaze. A smile played at the corner of her lips, and he wondered if she were actually intrigued.

Maybe she was as drunk as he.

"What did you have in mind?" she said at last. "I'm not going home with you. And I've had enough drinks."

Reed hesitated, his mind bogged down by indecision. He cleared his throat and motioned toward the stage. "Um . . . wanna dance?"

This time her laugh sounded genuinely amused. "This ain't that kind of club. I've got a better idea."

4

Reed followed Sirena through the tight crowd. She ducked and slipped between the sweaty bodies, occasionally pausing to return a high five or accept a drunken compliment. She moved with the grace and ease of an urban angel, her hips rocking with the beat of the music overhead. Her whole body seemed consumed by music. Even as she walked, it was still in her step. Every beat. Every riff.

The crisp air outside the club was a refreshing relief to the muggy confines of the cramped interior. Reed drew in a long breath and put his hands in his pockets. The glow of the skyline obscured most of the stars, but Sirena smiled as she stared upward.

Reed just watched her, feeling an involuntary smile tug at the corner of his mouth. She looked happy, and as soon as the thought hit him, he realized what a rare thing that actually was.

"I love the stars." Her comment seemed sudden and

conclusive, as though she didn't expect or really want a response.

Reed didn't break the moment. Instead, he looked back up at the sky and suddenly wished he could extinguish the city lights. Let the heavens take over.

He'd never wished for something like that before.

Sirena started for the parking lot.

"Let's take a ride."

Reed shifted on his feet, subconsciously adjusting the SIG where it hung in a shoulder holster beneath his shirt. She beckoned him on.

"Come on, cowboy. Don't get cold feet on me now. I wanna show you something."

Reed pulled his car keys from his pocket and turned toward the Camaro, but Sirena shook her head and walked in the other direction.

"Nope. I don't get into cars with strange men. We're taking mine."

Reed followed her down the line of parked SUVs, sedans, and pickup trucks. It looked like a used car lot.

"What if I don't get into cars with strange women?" he said.

"Well, you're in luck. I'm not strange. Crazy, but not strange. Hop in."

Reed followed her around the corner of a pickup and saw a yellow Volkswagen Beetle parked on the other side. It was old. Mid-seventies, at least, with hints of rust around the wheel wells and one missing hubcap. The roof featured a rusted luggage rack, tilted awkwardly toward the driver's side. Mud clung to the tires, and the headlights were misted over with age and erosion.

"This?" Reed couldn't hide his surprise.

Sirena unlocked the door and shrugged. "You can walk."

Reed hurried to the passenger side and piled in, cramming his six-foot-four-inch frame into the confines of the vintage economy car. Sirena landed beside him with a plop and poked the keys into the ignition. She depressed the clutch and tapped the gas pedal a couple times, then twisted the key. A dull clicking sound emanated from the rear of the car.

Sirena rolled her eyes. "Hold on."

She pushed past him and dug around in the back seat. The sound of paper crumbling was followed by metal clanking on metal. Sirena emerged with a hammer and retreated to the rear of the car. She banged around under the hood, then returned to the driver's seat and tossed the hammer into the back.

"Sorry. He does that sometimes."

"He?"

"Oscar. My car. He's old and crusty. But he loves me!"

This woman is crazy.

Reed lifted his hand for the door, but he didn't really intend to open it. She twisted the key, the motor coughed, and the engine roared to life. The little car vibrated as though it were about to fly apart, but it rolled forward with surprising grace and agility.

"I'm Banks, by the way."

Reed twisted in the narrow seat and frowned. "I thought your name was Sirena Wilder."

She laughed. "That's just a stage name. You know . . . to keep the crazies away. My real name is Banks Morccelli."

Reed wanted to point out that her real name sounded a great deal more contrived than her stage name, but somehow the comment didn't seem safe or welcome. Besides, there was something charming about the unusual name. He kind of liked it.

"Chris," he said. "Chris Thomas."

"A pleasure to meet you, Chris." Banks shifted into third gear and turned the Beetle onto the highway. "I may still call you cowboy. It fits your persona better."

"My persona?"

"Yeah, you know. Leaning up on the bar with all that swagger and condescension, judging the whole universe while you sip on a Jack and Coke and hit on the bartender. Cowboy."

He shot her a sideways look, wondering if she had randomly guessed his drink of choice or had observed him consuming it. Maybe Jen mentioned it.

"I'm not judging anyone," he said. A tinge of defensiveness rang in his voice, and he winced. He should have let it go.

Banks laughed. "Relax, dude. You're too serious. Roll your window down. It's stuffy in here."

He turned the crank on the door panel and lowered the tiny window. Banks followed suit, and the crisp fall air whistled through the little car. It felt amazing on his neck and bare forearms. Through the window, he watched the busy streets of south Atlanta pass by in a blur. Banks drove with aggression and very little grace, grinding each gear and swerving in and out of traffic. The small car would occasionally groan, and Banks would reach forward and pat the dash, poking her bottom lip out and talking to the vehicle directly.

A repressed gut instinct warned Reed that the behavior should alarm him, but he couldn't help finding it endearing. Banks seemed utterly lost in her little world—her windblown hair snapping back behind her ears as she careened around each turn. They pulled up next to a low-slung Monte Carlo at a red light, and the heavy beat of a rap track echoed across the intersection. Reed was surprised to see Banks turn toward the car and offer a "hang loose" gesture at its occupants before she broke out into an enthusiastic attempt at rapping along with the song.

It was terrible. Stifling a smile, Reed looked ahead as the Beetle groaned and bounced forward again, clearing another hill and winding into a residential section of the city.

"Where are we going?" he asked.

Banks shook her head. "Don't ask questions. Just enjoy the ride."

It was difficult to enjoy the ride when his head was continually slamming into the roof of the small car, but there was something enchanting about her careless flamboyance. He wondered how old she was. When he saw her on stage, he assumed she was in her early or mid-twenties, but now he wondered if she might still be a teenager.

Oscar bounced around another corner then slid to a stop in a small parking lot. A MARTA sign stood between the road and a set of train tracks. It read *Oakland City Station*.

Banks jerked the parking brake, then hopped out of the car. "Come on, cowboy!"

Reed pried himself out of the cabin and waited as Banks dug through the front trunk of the car. She emerged a few seconds later with a small case on backpack straps. She slung it over her shoulder, and they jogged across the street to the station. Reed bought a MARTA card while Banks leaned against the wall, humming and gazing up at the stars.

The train arrived a few minutes later, and Banks hopped on board. Reed hurried to follow, sliding in as the doors smacked shut behind him. The computerized voice of the prerecorded MARTA announcer rang through the car.

"This train is bound for the Doraville Station."

The train started forward with a rush, and Reed started to sit, but Banks grinned and shook her head.

"No. Here, stand in the middle. Now press your feet together. All the way. Yeah, like that. Now bend with the train."

As the momentum of the car climbed, Reed struggled to keep his balance. Banks giggled and swayed with the building g-force, her sneakers remaining planted on the dirty grey floor.

"Come on, cowboy. Ride the bronco!"

Reed couldn't resist a laugh. He stumbled backward and grabbed at the overhead rail. The train stopped at the next station, and Banks urged him to try again. Once more the car launched forward, and once more Reed stood in the middle of the floor with his feet planted together. As the momentum built, he leaned back and focused on maintaining his balance. Lights flashed past the windows, and the wheels clicked on the track underneath. Reed slipped and landed in the middle of the car.

Banks laughed and leaned against the wall.

"Damn, son. You've got the balance of a rolling stone."

Reed shrugged and grinned. His face was hot, and he grabbed the overhead rail. Why did his legs feel so stiff and awkward? He watched Banks as she slouched into a seat and pulled out her phone. Stations flashed past as her fingers clicked on the screen. The light from the phone reflected in her eyes, making her whole face glow. Kicked back in the dingy mass-transit seat, she looked as content with life as anyone he'd ever met.

The announcer rang overhead. "The next station is Lindbergh Center."

Banks jumped up and shoved the phone into her pocket. The train screeched to a halt. As the door slid open, she grabbed his hand. He hesitated and looked down. Her fingers were delicate, wrapped around his, but her grip was stronger than he anticipated.

She pulled his arm, laughing again. "Come on. This is it!"

They ducked through the door and onto the platform. Reed stumbled to keep up, and she led him across the street toward a five-story parking deck. He hesitated. A distant voice in the back of his head nagged him not to wander into a dark parking garage with a stranger. What could Banks possibly want to show him? Was this a setup? Had he misread everything about the pretty blonde?

He gritted his teeth and silenced the voice. He hated feeling cynical and seeing the devil around every corner. This moment was perfect, and he wouldn't ruin that with his practiced paranoia.

Banks pulled him into the garage. "Come on. Trust me."

She slipped past the ticket booth at the entrance of the first level and walked to the elevator. Punching the top floor button, she slumped against the wall and winked at him again.

"I don't get it," Reed said with a chuckle.

"Wait for it."

The elevator stopped at the top floor, and the doors rolled open. Reed stepped out onto the broad, open-air level, and shoved his hands into his pockets. He followed Banks toward the edge of the garage, drinking in deep breaths of the cold air as he watched her hips sway with each step. Even though the only sound in the sharp night air was the squeak of the departing train, Banks still walked as though she was in the middle of a thundering concert.

"Here. Look."

Banks stopped at the waist-high wall that ran around the perimeter of the garage.

Spread out before them, the Atlanta skyline shone beneath the clear black horizon. Each building stood in independent majesty, towering over the sleepy city, glowing champions of the night. The twin peaks of 191 Peachtree Tower glowed in amber glory from the powerful beacon lights nestled at its top. A few blocks away, the cylindrical glass mass of the Westin Peachtree Plaza rose eight hundred feet above street level, glimmering in the light of the other towers as guests slept quietly within its darkened rooms.

The soft glow of the skyline calmed Reed's nerves. He rested his hands against the wall and wondered why he'd never taken time to enjoy this view before. It was both breathtaking and tranquil.

Banks grabbed his shoulder and threw her leg over the wall.

Reed reached for her hand. "Hey! What are you doing?"

"Relax, doofus." She laughed and smacked his arm. "If I were gonna jump, it wouldn't be off a parking garage."

Banks pried his hand free and slung her leg over the wall, plopping down with her feet swinging in midair over the quiet street sixty feet below. She slapped the concrete beside her.

"Have a seat, cowboy."

Reluctantly, Reed slung his legs over the wall and sat down beside her. With a grin on her face, Banks unzipped her case and pulled out a ukulele strung with four plastic strings. It was just big enough to look comical.

She nestled the little instrument over her legs and gently strummed. The melodic sound was both louder and sweeter than Reed anticipated. He folded his arms and sat quietly as she started to sing.

"City lights, city skies. The only love I know, the only place I call home. Wherever I go, these lights hold my heart. They shine in my dark. They love me so."

The world fell still around him, and he watched her. Each twist of her small hand. Her wide, beautiful smile as she sang each line. It was as though he had vanished, and she was lost. Alone in a world that only she knew.

Strumming slowly, she gazed out at the skyline and sang just loud enough to carry a tune over the ring of the instrument. She repeated the song twice, singing softer each time.

Finally, the ukulele fell silent. Banks hugged it against her body and leaned forward, still gazing at the city. For a full five minutes, she just sat, staring at the lights and the gleaming towers. Huddled beside her on the edge of the wall, Reed just watched. Her shoulders, bare under the night breeze, were covered in goosebumps, but she didn't shiver.

Who is this woman?

Between hits, Reed enjoyed the occasional one-night stand. Once upon a time, he'd even had a girlfriend. But he never recalled wanting to know somebody like he wanted to know Banks, watching her right now. A grumpy old bulldog was his family, a dirty cabin his home, and he never minded that. Life was always about the next job—the next bloody checkmark on the hit list.

Get to thirty. Don't get killed. Don't get caught. Don't think too hard about it.

They were such dry, empty ambitions. Did Banks have ambitions? Did she dream at night of being free? Of not having a gun over her head? No. She already embodied freedom, as though nothing and nobody could ever tell her she wasn't alive and as free as the wind.

Maybe that's what I see. Maybe that's what I envy.

Banks looked up at him as though she knew his thoughts, then pulled him in and kissed him on the lips, gently. Reed's heart skipped and then rushed to life. His fingers trembled as he leaned into her. Her soft lips tasted of daiquiri.

God, she can kiss.

Banks drew back and slid her hand down his arm.

"Thanks, cowboy."

Reed sat a little stunned, unsure what to say. At last he mumbled: "For what?"

She poked him in the arm. "For shutting up and enjoying the view."

5

North Georgia

The cell phone's loud buzz woke Reed, and he shoved the blankets off his legs. A hint of sunlight glowed through the east-facing window of the cabin, but the living room was still dark. Quiet. Except for Baxter's snoring, of course. The big bulldog slept on his back in front of the stone fireplace, his legs sticking straight up in the air, his tongue lolling out the side of his mouth.

Reed rubbed the sleep out of his eyes and looked down at the phone.

O.E.

He hit the answer button. "Prosecutor."

It was his preassigned code name. All of Enfield's killers had one, and Enfield picked them himself. Reed earned the title because when he first started his career as an assassin for hire, he needed more than money to kill somebody. He needed a reason. Something to "prosecute" the victim for.

Enfield probably intended the name to be derogatory, but Reed owned it. It worked for him. Except now, after all these years . . . maybe he didn't search as hard for that reason as he used to. Maybe the fact that this person, whoever they were, stood between him and his freedom was reason enough to prosecute them.

"Reed. You never called."

Oliver's voice snapped just a little, jarring Reed back to the present. The older man's tone carried a mixture of annoyance and indifference, and Reed's stomach twisted, a hot lump welling up in his throat. There was no avoiding it now. "I was occupied."

Reed stumbled to his feet and climbed down the steps, accidentally tripping over Baxter on his way to the coffee machine. The big dog snorted and rolled to his feet, bursting into a chorus of barks and charging straight for the sliding glass door. He slammed face-first into the clean glass and stepped back, snorting and swaying on his stubby legs before he fell over sideways and commenced to snoring again.

Reed decided to let Oliver initiate the inevitable. "What do you need?"

"Are you drunk?" Oliver's tone softened a little, almost as if he gave a crap.

"No. Just a little hungover. I was out relaxing last night."

"You show your face too much, kid. It's gonna bite you in the ass one of these days."

Oliver was always saying things like that. Coming

from a man whom Reed had only met in person twice over the last three years, Reed wasn't too concerned with the judgment. He knew how to look after himself.

"Everybody needs a little fresh air, Oliver. You could use some yourself."

"I guess you deserved a drink. The client was very satisfied with your work up in Jersey. It should unlock quite a bit of future business for us."

Reed wasn't sure what to say to that; it was always strange discussing death in terms of sales and customers, as though Oliver were running a lemonade stand and struggling to discover the perfect balance of sweet and sour.

"Thank you." It was the only thing Reed could think to say.

"I understand you accepted a new job. The Atlanta hit."

"That's right. Just waiting on Brent to get me the file."

"Excellent. This is a big one, isn't it? Thirty?"

Here we go.

"That's right. This is thirty."

"That's great, Reed. I knew you'd do well, but I have to say you've impressed me. You're an incredible killer."

Reed leaned against the counter and picked up a bottle of whiskey. He took a long sip straight from the bottle and gazed out the front windows of the cabin. The sun rose over the Georgia pines, lighting up the surface of the forty-acre lake lying between the foothills. A glowing mist clung to the surface of the water as the sun began to burn it away.

Banks. He could still feel her kiss on his lips and smell her faint perfume. He could hear her voice and the melody of the ukulele. She left right after kissing him. She had flipped her legs back over the wall, poked him in the ribs, and winked. She'd said, "I like you, cowboy," and without a backward glance, she slung the ukulele over her shoulder and disappeared into the elevator.

Reed wanted to follow her. He wanted to chase her down, seduce her into spending the night with him. Somehow, he knew not to try.

"I think you should take a vacation."

Oliver's sudden comment jarred him out of the daydream, and Reed rubbed his eyes. "I'm glad you say that, Oliver. Actually—"

"You should check out the Caribbean. It's hot down there. Girls half-naked all the time. Get some drinks, bathe in the sun. Rent a sailboat. It's important to recharge. Keep your balance. You'll roll back in here twice the killer you left as."

This is it. I can't put it off any longer.

Reed set the bottle on the counter. "Oliver, I'm retiring. After this hit, I'm done. I fulfilled my end of the deal . . . I'm gonna walk."

The line fell silent. The hot lump returned to Reed's throat, and he shoved a cup under the spout of the coffee machine, watching while it filled. He dumped a healthy shot of whiskey into the mug, then stepped over Baxter and slid the door open.

When Oliver finally spoke, his tone was subdued

and soft. He almost sounded tired. "I'm disappointed, Reed."

The wicker rocking chair next to the door had seen better days. Reed eased into it and propped his feet on the porch rail, relishing the wave of relaxation that settled over his body. The coffee was scalding hot, but it felt good on his throat. For weeks he had dreaded this conversation, but now that it had come, he just wanted to plow ahead.

"I've worked hard, Oliver. I'm very grateful for what you've done for me, but a deal is a deal. I'm holding up my end; thirty kills. Then I walk."

"You're looking at this all wrong. Your contract was never meant to be terminal. Of course, you're free after thirty, but you've got a good thing going here. Your salary doubles now, and there are opportunities for advancement. You could run this company. You're that good. Don't walk away when you're just warming up."

Just warming up. Reed tried not to internalize that statement. Tried not to overthink the fact that this man had interpreted his bloody slew of twenty-nine kills as a warm-up for a greater, more catastrophic spree.

He forced himself to sip the coffee, staring at the lake. Then he leaned forward and set the cup on the wicker table beside him. "It's not something I'm willing to discuss. You saved my life. Gave me a second chance. I'll never forget that, but I'm finished after this job. I don't want a career."

Oliver spoke in a dull monotone. "Are you sure about that, Reed?"

"Yes. Absolutely."

His boss sighed. "You're a stubborn one, I'll give you that. I'm gonna be damn sad to see you go."

A tinge of remorse loosened the knot in Reed's stomach. This was the twisted, messed up part. He couldn't make himself view Oliver as evil. Objectively, his boss was the definition of evil. A man who made his living off the mass murder of others. A kingpin killer. And yet . . . and yet he had been there. When nobody else was. When Reed was facing death himself, alone, at the end of his rope. Oliver had been there.

"I'm very grateful for everything, Oliver. You've been good to me. It's just my time."

"If you're sure."

"I'm sure."

Oliver's voice snapped back to a confident, commanding tone. "All right, then. Let me know when you're done. I'll kick you a bonus for all the hard work."

Reed tapped the end-call button and finished the coffee. Baxter snorted from the other side of the open door, then stumbled out onto the porch for his usual scratch between the ears. He groaned and leaned against the wicker legs of the chair. Reed wondered if Oliver was anything like the old bulldog—tired, grouchy, and losing his edge.

He looked back over the lake and slumped into the chair. The faces of the twenty-nine people he had killed skipped across his memory, beginning with Paul Choc —the Latino man he killed while in prison. That kill sparked a series of events that led him here, twenty-eight kills later. That kill earned him an audience with Oliver Enfield, the kingpin assassin who offered to take

Reed off death row, spring him out of prison, and give him a second chance at life. All Reed had to do was kill twenty-nine more people.

Reed closed his eyes, and for the millionth time in his life, he wondered where it all went wrong. Was it when he joined the gangs of South Los Angeles as a teenager? Was that the first misstep? Or was it when he joined the Marines and trained to become an expert killer?

No. Being a Marine pulled him out of the ugly streets of South LA.

So what, then? He rested his head in his hands, letting his mind drift back to years before—years before death row, and prison, and all the brutal realities of being a professional assassin—all the way back to that fateful night in Iraq. He still remembered the way the rifle felt in his hand. The soft kick of the weapon as each bullet left the chamber. The way the men crumbled at the end of his gun, bleeding out in the sand.

That was the moment. Iraq was when everything changed.

Reed looked up, his eyes burning in the light of the rising sun. His body ached, and his brain throbbed. Every thought, every movement was a special sort of micro-agony. And yet . . .

I would do it again. I would gun them down without a second thought.

Reed rubbed his eyes and set down the cup, then patted Baxter on the rib cage. "As soon as I finish in Atlanta, we're gonna hit the road. I figure we can make Kansas City in a day, and then it's all wide-open highway to California. I've got enough cash set back for us to live on for years. We'll open up that garage and tinker with cars. Maybe find you a bitch."

Baxter snorted.

"Oh, come on," Reed said. "You know what I mean. A *female dog*."

The bulldog snorted again and waddled back into the house, leaving Reed alone on the porch. He lifted the phone back to his ear and heard it ring three times before the voicemail kicked in.

"Brent, it's Reed. Hurry up with the kill file. Thanks."

Back in the cabin, Reed retrieved the bottle of Jack and settled onto the low stool in front of his laptop on the kitchen table. With a few clicks on his keyboard, he navigated to Facebook. He never used it for personal applications, but maintained a couple fake profiles for research purposes—usually to investigate his next target.

Clicking over the search field, he typed "Banks Morchely" and hit the return key. The results were slim and mostly consisted of business pages for various community banks around the country. No personal profiles matched the beautiful blonde from the night before.

Reed took another sip of Jack and stared at the screen. He snapped his fingers and returned to the search bar. Maybe her last name was like Gucci—the *ch* sound was made with two C's.

Reed typed "Banks Morccelli" into the search field again and drummed his fingers on the table. The internet connection this far off the beaten path was shoddy at best.

A short listing of personal profiles joined the lineup of community banks. Reed scanned them, then allowed his mind to drift back through the haze of whiskey to the night before. He thought about her wide smile and bright blue eyes.

None of the pictures on his screen matched the memory.

Reed shut the laptop and stumbled to the kitchen, where he heated a skillet over the stove and opened a can of dog food. A clump of the food spilled onto the kitchen floor, and Baxter leered at it. Reed sighed and deposited the remainder of the food into the bulldog's bowl.

"Sorry, boy. Kinda hungover this morning."

After Baxter shoved his face deep into his breakfast, Reed returned to the skillet and cracked a couple eggs over the iron. As they began to bubble, he thought again about Banks's goofy, half-sly wink. Her stupid Volkswagen.

Reed reached for his phone, then stopped himself.

No. This was silly. He didn't have time for this. He had a job to do. The last job. There was no room for emotion right now.

If he hadn't been so drunk the night before, he never would have engaged with the singer, no matter how badly he wanted to. It was a pointless, reckless self-exposure. The kind of thing that got assassins killed.

Reed flipped the eggs onto a plate and dropped

three strips of bacon into the pan. Baxter appeared out of nowhere, sniffing and snorting. Reed smirked at him and tossed him a piece of raw bacon. The dog slurped it down like spaghetti, then collapsed onto the kitchen rug and began to snore again.

Reed stared down at his pet.

"She would like you," he mused. He wondered what Banks would say to the dog. Imagined how she would scratch him behind the ears and plop down on the floor beside him. Pull out the ukulele. Maybe sing a song about fat, grouchy dogs.

Reed wondered where she lived. If she had a boyfriend. If she was really from Mississippi, or if she was just passing through. Maybe she would head to Nashville or New York, keep singing, and become famous. Maybe he'd never see her again.

Reed dialed his phone, and a flat, toneless voice answered on the other end.

"Winter."

Reed didn't know if it was a man or a woman on the other end of the line. He never could tell. He didn't know Winter's ethnicity, or where Winter called home. In fact, he didn't know anything about the "analyst" who so often conducted his background checks, research projects, and scavenger hunts as he executed his diverse contracts. Winter was a ghost who knew all, yet couldn't be known. The ultimate eye in the sky. The omnipotent librarian.

If something was going down anywhere in the world, Winter knew about it. If somebody was missing or hiding, Winter could find them. If a whispered conversation took place in a bunker a mile underground, Winter could find out what was said.

Winter wasn't a person. Winter was a force of nature. Hence the name, maybe.

"I need you to pull a file for me," Reed said. "A person."

"Whose account do I charge?" Winter's voice was as toneless and neutral as ever.

"Mine. This isn't a contract. It's personal."

"Very well. What's the name?"

"Banks Morccelli. Female. American. Currently residing in Decatur, Georgia. I think."

Reed heard Winter scratching on a notepad.

"What do you want to know?" The voice sounded more than a little cryptic.

"I'm not sure. Just . . . if she's a real person. Or an alias. Whatever you can find."

"Very well. I'll be in touch."

The phone clicked. Reed chewed his bottom lip as he stared out the glass door again. The phone call made him feel like a stalker, and for all intents and purposes, maybe he was.

But it didn't matter. He had to know.

6

B rent called back fifteen minutes later to inform Reed the kill file was available on his secure email drive. The broker's typical charisma sounded muted, as though he were sick.

The email drive Reed used for work was triple-encrypted and housed on an international server. It wasn't impregnable, but isolated enough to minimize casual governmental surveillance.

He opened the file and scanned the contract. $35,000 for the successful assassination of Mitchell Holiday, without any link to the contracting party. An additional $5,000 paid as a rush fee to complete the job in the next seventy-two hours, and a $15,000 bonus for a "conspicuous prosecution of contract, rendering the target maliciously slain by intentional methods."

In layman's terms, they wanted it to be messy.

The contract was pretty standard, and the compensation was acceptable, but that last footnote, that appeal for a graphic execution, bothered Reed. It wasn't unusual to receive a special request regarding the method of death, and there was usually some form of qualifier or requirement tacked onto the contract. The last agreement requested that he mask the scene from any indicators of a professional hit, which was why he burned the boat and left the gun in his victim's hand. If any evidence remained after the boat sank, none of it would point back to a third party's involvement.

The request for a conspicuous and rushed death was both atypical and concerning, however. It indicated an emotional decision to kill made by somebody who was either rash or desperate. Rash and desperate people were dangerous. They made poor choices, defaulted on payment, and were an absolute liability if they became cornered by the police. The payment wouldn't be a problem—Brent always collected in advance. But something about the hit felt wrong. It was too . . . forced.

Reed scrolled past the outline and stopped at the target profile—Mitchell Thomas Holiday. State senator for Georgia's third district, covering the Atlantic Coast south of Savannah. He held an MBA from Vanderbilt University and owned a thriving logistics company based out of his hometown of Brunswick. Holiday was single, with no ex-wives or children. He was handsome, in his late forties, and had thick, salt-and-pepper hair, a good build, and the kind of smile that won elections— eight of them, ranging in significance from Brunswick town council, to the mayor of Brunswick, and then state senator. This was to be his last term. He had already announced his intention to retire and focus on "other pursuits," although a few pundit blogs named him as a potential candidate for governor.

Reed leaned back and rubbed his chin with one thumb as he stared at the picture.

"What did you do, Mitch? Why do they want you dead?"

Come on, Reed. Not this again. Just cap the SOB, and you're done. It doesn't matter why they want him dead.

Still, he couldn't help but feel a twinge of something in the pit of his stomach. Was it curiosity or foreboding? It was difficult to tell the difference.

The third page listed specific information about Holiday's habits and residence. Not surprisingly, Holiday owned a house in Brunswick, a vacation cabin in North Carolina, and a condominium in downtown Atlanta, which he used while the general assembly was in session. The Senate was in session for another few days, which meant Holiday should be in town.

After memorizing the downtown address, Reed shut the computer and twisted his neck until it popped. He'd take a trip downtown to do some scouting and formulate a plan.

He had seventy-two hours, one press of the trigger . . . and it would all be over.

The Camaro purred like a jungle cat as Reed directed it around the gentle curves of Highway 9 out of

Dawsonville. Dawson County was beautiful in late October, with amber leaves drifting down off the foothills and blowing across the asphalt. In spite of the shedding trees, it was warm, and Reed drove with the windows down, enjoying the rumble of the motor and the touch of October on his face.

The foothills faded into city streets, and the Atlanta skyline loomed on the horizon. Small subdivisions and urban townhomes passed on either side, festooned with plastic skeletons, tree-hung ghosts, and Styrofoam tombstones. Halloween was the following day, and the city was fully engaged in the haunted trappings of the creepy holiday. Reed found the celebratory application of death and doom to be relentlessly ironic. Every year, as Halloween swept across the country, he marveled at the millions of Americans who embraced a cartoonish version of death with all the zeal and commercialization they invested into Christmas. He didn't judge them for it. How could they know how churlish the production looked through the eyes of a professional killer? Maybe he envied them and their simple joys and guarded innocence. What would it be like to laugh about fake blood on the floor and to dress up as a grim reaper? Would they laugh as much if they knew how close death might be?

He parked the car at MARTA's North Springs Station and took the train into the city, feeling a strange twinge in the pit of his stomach as he passed Lindbergh Center. It wasn't the first time he kicked himself for letting her walk away. He should have stopped her.

Asked for her number. Talked her into returning home with him.

No. Something told him Banks wouldn't have fallen for that. Was she too smart, or just not interested? He couldn't be sure. And now, unless Winter could pull her out of thin air, he might never find out.

Maybe that was best. A gut instinct nagged at the edge of his consciousness, reminding him that attachment was the fast lane to getting himself killed or imprisoned. Again. How would this random infatuation serve him after his last contract? Banks couldn't come with him, and he wasn't sticking around Atlanta. There would be a girl in Idaho or Utah or wherever he finally landed; a girl who would meet the new Reed, a racing mechanic with a boring background and no greater ambitions than a house in the mountains and football on the weekends; a subdued Reed who laid his demons in a mile-deep grave before shoveling concrete over their faces.

What would it be like to have somebody?

Reed rested his head against the vibrating window of the train and pictured himself in a house by the mountains. Maybe there was a big garage with four or five cars to tinker with. Baxter was there, of course. And . . . somebody. When he pictured the house in the hills with snowcapped mountains in the backdrop, it was easy to slip Banks into the rocking chair next to his. Was that because her face was so fresh in his memory? She wasn't the first woman he'd felt sparks with. There had been one other, years before. She was a professional car thief, and they met by sheer chance in the midst of a hit. The whirlwind romance that followed over the next six weeks was overwhelming, but from the outset, Reed knew it wasn't the sort of thing forever and always was made of. Kelly was spontaneous, reckless, and exciting. But she wasn't the type of woman he could picture in the rocking chair. He couldn't imagine her scratching Baxter's ears or strumming a guitar as the sun set.

Could he picture Banks in that chair? Did it matter?

Get yourself together, Reed. This girl is stuck in your head.

Reed shook away the thoughts of Banks and departed the train at the Arts Center Station. He didn't have time for daydreams. What was that old chestnut his mother used to preach at him? Something about carts and horses—doing things in the order they should be done. First, Holiday. Finish his contract and claim his freedom, then leave Georgia behind. Build a new identity and a new life thousands of miles away. Then there would be time for all the other big gaps in his life.

He took a cab from the train station to The Foundry Park due north of town. Mitchell Holiday owned a condominium on the fourteenth floor of The Atlantic —a forty-six floor high-rise situated at 270 17th Street. Interstate 85 was less than a mile to the east, and directly across the street was a small outlet mall sandwiched between the park and the freeway. The Millennium Gate Museum stood down the street next to a small duck pond, bringing a touch of the serene to an otherwise bustling part of the city.

Reed paid the cab driver in cash and pulled a Carolina Panthers hat low over his ears before walking toward the shopping mall. He tossed occasional glances toward the high-rise, acclimating himself to the curvature of the exterior glass and the exposed framework of the post-modern building. It was beautiful, really. Exactly the kind of place a person with a healthy salary would select in North Atlanta. Not quite Buckhead, but not quite Midtown, either. A happy medium for a man who was only home a few short hours each night.

For the next hour, while settled on a metal park bench near the duck pond, Reed observed each person who passed. Locals walked dogs along the path. A crew of landscapers worked on a fall flower bed next to the museum. A mother duck and her ducklings waddled next to the waterline, quacking and butting into each other.

What do you call a mother duck? A hen? That doesn't sound right.

Reed looked up at The Atlantic. Through the glare on the tinted glass, he could just make out the silhouettes of residents bustling back and forth on the inside. Holiday's unit number indicated that it was on the fourteenth floor, but Reed didn't know which side of the building it was on. It would be a trick to figure that out without entering the building, and he wanted to avoid that if possible. There would be cameras, concierges, and old women with oversized handbags—too many people who might remember him later.

Reed dug a cigarette out of his coat pocket and chewed on the end, pondering his options. The most obvious place to isolate Holiday would be at his home. At the Capitol, there was a plethora of security personnel, cameras, metal detectors, and witnesses. Also, the Capitol was situated just south of downtown in a busy district with lots of red lights and one-way streets. It would be incredibly difficult to make a getaway without being trapped amid the traffic. Certainly, it would be conspicuous to kill Holiday on the Capitol steps, but given the right method of execution and the proper dramatic flair, any death would be conspicuous once CNN had their way with it.

The second option would be to hit Holiday someplace open and exposed between home and work. A sports bar or a train station. Someplace where the hit could be lightning quick with a clean getaway and minimal security. Such an arrangement was ideal, and it was how Reed conducted most of his hits: learn his target's patterns and habits, identify an opportunity, and then strike out of the shadows.

The problem with option two was the timing. With less than seventy-two hours to monitor Holiday's daily habits and become accustomed to the places he visited, it would be difficult—almost impossible—to identify an opportunity to make a safe and effective hit. It would require a stroke of dumb luck to hit Holiday without exposing himself. There just wasn't enough time to study the patterns.

That left option three, which was to hit Holiday at home. The high-rise offered minimal security compared to the Capitol, and Holiday's whereabouts would be easy to predict and exploit. Given only a few hours of research, Reed could locate Holiday's unit, identify an ideal method of execution, and begin planning his escape. Holiday would be home at night, providing the cover of darkness and lighter traffic for easier extraction. The cherry on top would be the horrific nature of a senator being executed in his own home. If that wasn't conspicuous, Reed didn't know what was.

Reed shuffled down the sidewalk, still glancing at the building and zeroing in on the fourteenth floor. Every unit had windows, so one side of the building had to offer an exposed view into Holiday's condo. Reed circled the building twice, examining every angle of the fourteenth floor before he realized he was making this way harder than it had to be.

He punched Holiday's address and unit number into Google on his phone and was rewarded with a Zillow listing. The condo last sold in 2016 for $428,980. The listing contained details of the unit, including square footage, a floor plan, and pictures from the inside.

One of the pictures featured the giant wall-to-wall window that framed one side of the kitchen/living room/dining room combo. Zooming in on the picturesque view allowed him to focus on the landmarks. In the distance was a flagpole featuring a small blue flag with a yellow cross. Reed studied the flag, rotated the image, then looked up and scanned the horizon. Several hundred yards away, a blue spec flew a few feet beneath a giant American flag, mounted on top of a building.

Ikea.

Reed retraced his line of sight back toward the high-rise and settled on the fourteenth floor.

"Gotcha."

7

I t was a short jog to the Ikea. Reed approached the building from the north side and then turned to get a bearing on the high-rise. It stood in clear view, with no obstructing trees or buildings.

He glanced around the perimeter of the Ikea, checking for cameras, security guards, or foot traffic. The parking lot held a smattering of pickup trucks and minivans, but no police, no golf-cart security, and no rent-a-cop on a Segway.

When he made it to the rear of the building, Reed scanned the loading dock for any surveillance. The alley was quiet and littered with stray paper trash and puddles of oily runoff water. Past the loading dock, along the rear of the store, a dumpster overflowed with cardboard boxes, and directly next to it, an access ladder for the roof clung to the side of the building, its lowest rung hanging ten feet off the ground.

Reed hoisted himself onto the dumpster, and as his shoe squished against the damp edge, he slipped and then dug his fingers into the cold steel to keep from falling. He slowly rose to his feet, taking care to maintain his balance this time, and focused on the ladder.

It was mounted to the wall, four feet away, and about a foot up. After bracing himself agains the block wall of the building, he jumped, reaching out with both arms for the bottom rung. Reed missed the rung, but his hands closed around the man cage that surrounded the ladder, and he winced as the metal bit into his skin. Flakes of rust rained down over his face and into his mouth. As his legs dangled over the concrete and the full strain of his weight descended on his biceps, something in his shoulder popped. No matter how many hours he spent in the gym, he always found a way to pull a muscle and wake up sore. Reed let go with his right hand and grabbed the lowest rung of the ladder, then began to pull himself upward.

Yeah. This was gonna hurt later.

The roof was covered in pea gravel and humming air-conditioning units, and a few spots were patched with tar. At the northeast corner of the building, Reed dropped to his stomach and crawled the last twenty feet to the edge of the roof.

An eighteen-inch parapet surrounded the building, blocking his view beyond. Reed positioned himself onto his knees, then kept his head low as he approached the brink. The sun beat down on the white-painted blocks of the parapet, and Reed shielded his eyes to view the high-rise standing to the east of the duck pond.

From a small case in his cargo pants, he withdrew a

digital range finder. It was black, with a magnified scope and an invisible laser which would determine the distance to any object it was pointed at, within fifteen-hundred yards or so. He held the viewfinder to his eye, feeling just a hint of adrenaline rush into his blood. This was it—the journey leading up to the press of the trigger—the suspense and cold calculation. It wasn't about the blood, and it certainly wasn't about the money. It was about pushing himself to the edge, facing death, and ushering another human toward it. It was horrific, gritty—the rawest emotional experience Reed had ever felt. He couldn't tell the difference between dread and anticipation anymore, but he didn't like the feeling. Sure, there were moments when he sat behind the rifle, stared through the scope, and felt like God himself. But that high brought a brutal hangover of darkness and despair directly behind it, reassuring him that the cost wasn't worth the power trip.

The range finder offered him a clear view of the high-rise. Reed focused the crosshairs on the four-teenth floor of the building, then depressed the trigger on the side of the scope, activating the laser. A split second later, the range was displayed in front of the crosshairs—745 yards. An easy shot.

Reed lowered the range finder and studied the high-rise. It wasn't quite square with his position. He viewed Holiday's window from a forty-degree angle, which wasn't ideal; it limited his view of the interior of the condo, and there was a chance Holiday wouldn't expose himself at all.

On the other hand, the roof of the Ikea offered

unique advantages. When the coast was clear, he could enter and vacate at his convenience. There would be almost no chance of anyone else climbing to the roof after dark. Other than a handful of security cameras mounted on the light poles in the parking lot, all of which were pointed down, there was no electronic surveillance anywhere. Visually, he would be covered.

Audibly, the Ikea was also advantageous. The humming A/C units would provide moderate masking for a suppressed rifle. Contrary to what Hollywood seemed to believe, silencers didn't reduce the blast of a high-powered rifle cartridge to a puny pop. Even with a state-of-the-art suppression canister, the rifle would still make substantial noise. The A/C units, along with the vehicles in the parking lot, would help. The sound could be excused as a car backfiring or a runaway cart crashing into a minivan. An oblivious civilian wouldn't notice.

Last, there really wasn't another vantage point within range on this side of the high-rise. He could use a van or find a way to disguise his position in a park, but the odds of being caught in such an arrangement were much higher, and the field of view wouldn't be any better.

Ikea was the spot. He would set himself up a few yards behind the parapet and use a shooting mat and a bipod. A kill shot from an unseen assassin while the senator relaxed in his own home would be theatrical, and Reed would have ample time to get lost before the police arrived.

He popped his neck and returned the range finder

to its case. He checked the alleyway before hurrying down the ladder and cat-dropping the final ten feet onto the pavement.

It was a Thursday, and the senator would be home sometime after dark. Reed would return to the roof with his rifle and find a place he could conceal himself on the off chance somebody joined him. The glass on the side of the high-rise was reinforced; it wouldn't stop the bullet, but it wouldn't shatter, either. With any luck, Reed would be miles away before anyone knew Holiday was dead.

Breakfast was the last meal Reed had eaten, and nausea began to set in. Packaged beef jerky and can of Coke from a gas station was a poor substitute for a meal, but it would have to suffice. Reed fumbled in his pocket for his wallet.

"That'll be five-sixty."

He nodded and checked his left pocket. Did he leave it in the car? There was spare cash in his tennis shoe, but he really didn't want to dig that out in front of the cashier.

"Think I left my wallet in the car. It'll just be a minute."

"I got you, brother," came a voice behind him.

Reed looked over his shoulder. Behind him stood a short man with a tangled beard, holding a ten-dollar bill in his right hand. He wore torn jeans and a faded Falcons hoodie that was at least a size too large.

"Excuse me?"

The man grunted and set a bottle of water and a pouch of peanuts on the counter, then handed the cashier his ten. "Semper Fi. I got this one."

Reed frowned and shook his head at the cashier, but the half-stoned teenager was already poking the bill into the cash register.

"Semper Fi?"

Reed accepted the Coke and jerky from the man, who then smiled and gestured toward Reed's right forearm, where an Eagle, Globe, and Anchor tattoo was drawn in red ink. Reed pulled the sleeve of his jacket over the tattoo and grunted.

"Let me go to my car. I'll get you your money."

The man snorted and brushed dirty hair out of his face. "Seriously, dude. I got it. Jarheads stick together."

Reed shrugged and turned toward the door. "Well, thanks. Have a good one."

As he pushed through the door back into the crisp fall air, he heard the short man shuffling behind him. "Hey, you got a smoke on you? I was gonna buy a pack, but I'm a little light on cash."

Reed sighed and dug in his pocket. He handed the man a cigarette and then started to walk away again.

"Light?"

Reed stopped half step. He crammed his hand back into his pocket, dug the lighter out, and then waited as the dirty man rolled the smoke between his fingers, dangling the tip over the golden flame.

"You look like an infantryman," the man said. "Am I right?"

"Something like that."

"I was transport. You know, the shmucks in the trucks. Two tours in Iraq. All that jazz. You?"

Reed waved his hand. "Look, man, I'm in a rush. Just keep the lighter."

The dirty man nodded. "All right. Catch you la—"

Before he could finish, a snapping sound rang out from his right leg, and he toppled forward with a grunt of pain, catching himself on the edge of a newspaper dispenser before hitting the sidewalk. Reed lunged forward and caught him by the shoulder, then helped him up. The man gritted his teeth as he leaned back against the wall.

"You okay?" Reed asked.

He grunted, then took a drag of the cigarette. "Yeah. Just my leg. It's prosthetic from the knee down. The joint keeps breaking. I'll take care of it."

Reed looked down to a dirty and worn shoe, now twisted on the end of the man's right leg, looking ready to fall apart. Through the torn canvas, Reed saw a glint of the rusting metal prosthetic, and ripped jeans exposed more of the damaged mechanical appendage.

Reed cursed under his breath. "What happened there?"

"What you think happened? IED in Baghdad."

"You didn't get disability pay?"

He snorted. "You kidding me? I was somewhere I wasn't supposed to be doing something I wasn't supposed to be doing for people who weren't supposed to be giving orders. The VA considered it 'reckless endangerment.' I get three hundred bucks a month."

It wasn't the first such story Reed had heard. Not all the refugees from the Middle East were Middle Eastern.

"Wait here." Reed hurried around the corner and ducked behind a dumpster. He pried his shoe off, lifted the insole, and withdrew five hundred-dollar bills folded neatly together in a flattened wad.

Back around the building, he handed the cash to the slouching vet.

"Here. Go find yourself a shower and some fresh clothes. And for God's sake, get a haircut. You're way out of regs, my friend."

The vet glowered at the money for a long moment, then slowly reached out his right hand. Reed accepted the firm and confident handshake, simultaneously slipping him the cash.

"Sergeant Vincent Russel," he said. "My friends just call me Vince."

"Corporal Reed Montgomery . . . Force Recon."

Vince raised an eyebrow. "Force Recon? No kidding. Reckon your retirement is a helluva lot better than mine."

"Not when you retire in handcuffs." Reed's voice was flat, emotionless.

Vince crammed the bills into his pocket. "Well, then. I guess that's two things we have in common."

"Two things?" Reed cocked his head.

Vince jutted his chin toward Reed's untucked shirt and wrinkled jacket. "Yeah. You're also out of regs."

"Regs are overrated, aren't they?" Reed smirked. "Roll easy, Sergeant."

8

North Georgia

W inter's report waited in Reed's inbox when he returned to the cabin. The single email was labeled with nothing but a capital "W" in the subject line, and in spite of his resolve to leave Banks behind, fresh anticipation and a million questions flooded his mind. Had Winter found her? Who was she? Was anything she told him true? Perhaps the most important question wasn't about Banks . . . maybe it was about himself. Why did he need to know so much? Why did he feel so obsessed over the blonde singer with the ukulele? It was petty . . . childish . . . irresistible.

The first page was blank. The next contained half a dozen color photographs, and he recognized the girl in the pictures. Blonde. Long, swept-back bangs. Bright blue eyes. That intoxicating smile. Banks stood next to an older woman in one photo, and they favored one another. Perhaps it was her mother. Another picture showed her cuddling a black cat on a couch. She smiled while the cat slept.

Reed's fingers felt numb over the mouse pad. Banks was even more beautiful than he remembered, and even more intoxicating curled up on the couch without makeup.

Reed blinked and reached for the whiskey. He took a deep swallow and scrolled to the next page. Her full name was Banks April Morccelli. Born January 14, 1994, so she was a couple years his junior and older than she looked. He was relieved that she wasn't nineteen.

Her home address was an apartment in Decatur, where she lived alone. A 1972 Super Beetle was registered in her name, with three unpaid parking tickets linked to the plate number. Her phone number and email address were both listed, but under the social media tab, Winter had typed "No accounts found."

She's a performer. Why would a performer not have social media accounts?

As he scrolled down a little farther, he learned Banks was employed at a coffee shop in Buckhead. She graduated high school from a public school in rural Mississippi and dropped out of college at Ole Miss. Her passport expired four years ago, and before Decatur, her last known residence was another apartment in Memphis, where she lived for three months.

The next page was labeled "Financials." Reed scanned the tiny notations. Banks held a checking account with a regional bank, and it was overdrawn two hundred and forty dollars. She had over four thousand dollars of unpaid medical bills in collections, her power bill was past due, and she hadn't filed taxes in two years.

Beneath the financial tab were specifics on her medical record, including two hospitalizations in the previous twelve months. Prescriptions were written for various heavy-duty antibiotics. She had Lyme disease and no medical insurance.

Winter's reconnaissance was, as always, highly detailed. Reed wasn't sure what he was looking for when he requested the file, but he wasn't expecting the graphically clear picture that was painted before him: A girl on her own, barely scraping by, and struggling with significant medical conditions. No apparent friends or family to lean on, and no career or place to call home.

He hadn't seen any of that the night before. He would have never guessed her to be broke and alone, let alone chronically sick. She seemed so happy and colorful, as though nothing in the world could dim her glow. That made her all the more irresistible.

Walk away, Reed. Nothing in this file changes reality. This isn't the time or the woman. Walk away, now.

Reed pushed away the commanding voice in his head and unlocked his phone. It rang once before a friendly female voice answered.

"Lasquo Financial."

"The summer is hot, but at least it won't rain."

"There could be earthquakes," she answered without hesitation.

"Sure, but I have insurance."

"Thank you, sir. How may I direct your call?"

"Get me Thomas Lancaster, please."

"May I ask who's calling?"

"Reed Montgomery. Account ID 4871994."

"One moment, please."

A familiar voice with just a hint of a Cajun warble answered the line.

"Good afternoon, Reed. How are you today?"

Thomas Lancaster was the senior banker for Lasquo Financial, an independent corporation that housed a network of banking services to support the needs of the criminal underworld. The word on the street was that Lasquo was headquartered in New Orleans, but nobody actually knew for sure. Every time Reed's call was routed through their maze-like connection service, it was eventually matched with a new area code in a new city. Today it was area code 775—Reno, Nevada, which was further proof that the company was as ghostly as the people it served. While the money itself was doubtlessly stored in an assortment of Swiss, Grand Cayman, and third-world banks, Lasquo provided the daily conveniences that enabled contract criminals to exchange payments, invest in the stock market, and hide their illegal wealth. It was an orchestrated masterpiece designed to circumvent federal oversight by framing itself as a financial concierge service for elite businessmen. Reed wasn't exactly sure how it worked, and he didn't really care.

"Hello, Thomas. Another day in paradise. Could you pull my balance, please?"

"Sure. Liquid assets?"

"Just the checking is fine."

Reed heard the click of a computer keyboard.

"You have one million, two hundred twenty-two thousand, four hundred eight dollars, and forty-two cents available."

"Outstanding. I guess a payment came in?"

"Thirty-nine thousand, last night. From your last contract."

"Perfect. I'd like to make a wire, please."

"Of course. To which bank?"

"Uhm . . . it's some regional institution. Let me find it."

Reed read off the name of the bank while Thomas continued to tap on his keyboard.

"The beneficiary?"

"Banks Morccelli."

"How much would you like to send?"

"Twenty-five thousand."

"I'll have that out within the hour."

"Great. And Thomas, I'd like it to be anonymous. Is that possible?"

Thomas grunted. "Is the beneficiary not expecting the deposit?"

"No. And I don't want them to question it."

"Hmm . . . well, it's no trouble to make it untraceable. But I suspect that your average person who saw an unexpected deposit would assume it's an error and call the bank. I'll do what I can."

"That's fine. Thanks."

Reed heard the banker mumble something about wire fees, but he wasn't listening. He hung up and stared at Banks's picture. She was everything he remembered. All the grace and charm and charisma glowed just as brightly in the photo as it had under the nightclub lights. Was it wrong to pry into somebody's life? The question hit him like a bucket of ice water over his face. He'd never asked a question like that before, and why should he? Whenever he read a file like this, he was usually about to kill somebody. Digging through a sock drawer with noble intentions was virgin territory, let alone handing out money. Sure, he doled out his share of monthly guilt payments to an assortment of charities, but he never gave money to a specific person. It made him too accessible. Too vulnerable.

He thought about Vince, the homeless Marine at the gas station, and the money he gave him. This would be twice in one day that he made an erratic decision to step outside of his orchestrated comfort zone. It was dangerous, and it exposed him. It built connections he couldn't afford to have. Each relationship was a point of weakness in a carefully crafted armor of detached invincibility.

Armor that keeps me alone.

9

Atlanta, Georgia

T he sky was dark and cloudless. The parking lot of the Ikea emptied slowly, and Reed waited two hundred yards away in the Camaro, watching every person who left the building. He had arrived three hours before and surveyed the parking lot, surrounding streets, and passing cars, watching every face, every police cruiser, and searching for any red flags in the quiet urban landscape.

Reed was uncomfortable with pulling off a kill so quickly. He didn't feel prepared. He didn't know the terrain and moving parts well enough. A week of surveillance would have put his mind at ease.

Chill out, Reed. It's just another job—an easy one. The last one.

Reed left the Camaro across the street from the rear of the Ikea, parked in an empty lot with no security cameras or nearby structures. He shouldered a canvas bag and walked back into the alleyway behind the store. The shadows under the moon melded with his black pullover and cargo pants, helping him to blend into the alley and fade from view.

He had learned long ago that the key to sneaking around in a public, civilian environment was not to sneak. Find out where the people are, do your best to avoid them. Act casual, and dodge any professional security or surveillance devices. The rest tended to take care of itself.

Reed stuck his arm through the bag's shoulder strap, then repeated his jump from the dumpster to catch the bottom rung of the ladder. Five seconds later, he slid over the parapet and dropped onto the gravel below. The roof was dark and still hummed with the rhythmic purring of the air conditioners. Even with the chill outside, the interior of the store would quickly become stuffy without the steady ventilation from the A/C units. Reed had counted on that.

He squatted on the roof next to the ladder and listened. The Atlanta skyline glimmered, and his stomach twisted as he remembered the last time he enjoyed that view. It was less than twenty-four hours before, but it felt like days.

Gravel crunched under his boots as he ran toward the edge of the roof. The air was thick and heavy, and his clothes clung to his body, glued by a thin layer of sweat. The moonlight that illuminated the roof outlined a handful of air conditioner units. They purred in the darkness like sleeping cats, providing just enough noise to mask the scrape of his knees against the gravel as he knelt at the edge of the roof. He set a small digital anemometer on the parapet, then drew a deep breath of damp Georgia air. It tasted like city smog.

The anemometer swiveled on its mount until it faced the wind, and the little blades whirred to the hum of the air-conditioning units. Reed crawled back to the bag. After unrolling the shooting mat across the roof, his hands moved in a practiced blur as he withdrew the rifle and locked the barrel into the receiver. He knew every part of the weapon better than he knew himself. The polymer magazine was loaded with twenty rounds of .308. The smooth, aluminum trigger guard curled around the stainless steel, three-pound competition trigger. Known as a thousand-yard rifle due to its average effective range, Reed knew the weapon was capable of slightly more. But tonight, he needed less than eight hundred.

Reed pulled the lens caps off either end of the scope and twisted the power switch. His vision blurred momentarily against the red glow of the crosshairs. He settled down behind the rifle and lifted it into his shoulder, enjoying the familiar touch of the stock against his cheek. For the first time since leaving the car, he allowed himself to relax. With his eyes closed, he focused on loosening each muscle group—his back, legs, shoulders, and stomach—drawing in deep breaths and remaining perfectly still.

Tension faded from his body with each breath, and a calm settled over his mind like a cloud passing over the sun on a hot day. This was his silent place—the moment when distractions and stressors were excommunicated from his mind, and total focus took control. It was a whole-body experience that was more than just embracing the rifle; it was the moment he became part of the weapon.

Reed laid his trigger finger against the trigger guard and gazed through the scope. The dull lights of the shopping mall illuminated his view, and he pivoted the gun to the right until the crosshairs glided across The Atlantic. The parapet blocked his view of the ground, so he counted down from the top of the building, subtracting thirty-two floors before he rested the crosshairs over the fourteen level, then twisted the zoom control to the 30x mark.

The windows of Holiday's corner unit were dark, but through the crystal-clear glass of the powerful optic, Reed could discern the outlines of furniture parked around the living room. Something gleamed beyond the living area—maybe the clock on a microwave or stove.

The fan blades of the anemometer still spun silently, and the LCD read six knots from the southwest. The breeze was barely detectable and would have little impact on a shot at 745 yards, but it was still useful information. The wind might pick up speed or change direction, and a miscalculation could easily lead his bullet off target.

Reed settled back into the stock of the rifle, pressing his cheek against the polymer and resuming his surveillance of the condo. Now there was nothing to do but wait, and hope Holiday showed up.

Hours passed, and the parking lot of the Ikea was desolate, with only a handful of cars still gathered around the front entrance. The wind picked up for a while, then died off completely, leaving the night calm, though Reed wished it would return. A steady breeze could certainly make his shot more difficult, but it provided additional masking for the blast.

Reed lay perfectly still behind the rifle, his left eye shut, and his right eye focused on the condo. Every couple of minutes, he completed a sweep of the entire building and the sidewalk around it. Residents walked their dogs. Men watched TV. Women chatted on phones. Kids played video games. A young couple made love in a shadowy bedroom. None suspected that somebody might be watching them, let alone through the scope of a high-powered rifle.

Refocused on Holiday's condo, Reed checked his watch. It was almost ten o'clock. Holiday might be out at dinner or visiting with friends. Reed wanted to catch him right as he returned home, preferably in the living room where he would be most exposed. One shot to the base of the skull. Avoid the mess of trying to tap him in the bedroom, which was less visible.

A light flashed from somewhere inside the condo, and Reed's muscles tensed. As the kitchen light flooded his optic, somebody crossed his field of view. It was a man, tall and handsome, wearing a light grey jacket and a Braves baseball cap.

Without looking away from the scope, Reed

retrieved a car alarm transmitter from his bag, flipped a switch, and was answered by a barely audible beep. It was a universal device, programed to transmit a blast of constantly changing signals until one of them matched a car's emergency system.

Holiday bustled around the kitchen, smiling and talking on his cell phone. He poured himself a glass of wine and took a long sip. The crosshairs rose and fell over the senator with Reed's every gentle breath. Holiday brought his drink into the living room and flipped on the overhead light. Once Reed's eyes adjusted, he saw Holiday sitting on the couch with one leg crossed over the other, still on the phone, and taking sips of wine between animated laughs.

Reed pressed his thumb against the bolt-release button mounted on the left side of the receiver. The stainless-steel bolt slid forward over the magazine, stripping off the top round, and slamming it into the chamber. He disengaged the safety and set his left hand on the remote while holding the rifle into his shoulder with his right.

Holiday's left side was perfectly exposed to the crosshairs. Reed could make out the basic features of his face. The powerful curve of his left shoulder. The wrinkles in his jacket.

Reed lowered the crosshairs until they hovered over the base of Holiday's skull. He reached up and adjusted the windage and elevation knobs on the scope, ensuring the optic was calibrated correctly for the distance.

Holiday set down the phone and grabbed the TV

remote. The room flashed as the big flat-screen came to life. Reed wrapped his hand around the grip of the rifle, rested his finger against the trigger guard, then reached down and pressed a button on the transmitter. The device beeped again, and four seconds passed. Then the parking lot below erupted with the blaring of a car horn.

Reed pressed his face against the stock of the rifle and laid his finger against the trigger. He counted silently and matched the beat of the car horn with the tempo of his mind. He would fire on the third blast.

His finger tightened around the trigger, and the crosshairs fell still over Holiday's neck as Reed drew in a half-breath and held it. His world outside the scope blurred from existence, failing to matter anymore. Only the target mattered, and the inevitable moment when that target would crash to the floor.

The horn blared. Once. Twice.

Holiday turned toward the door and smiled. Reed felt the muscles in his chest tense. Something was wrong, he could feel it in the way Holiday's shoulders rose, and his eyes flashed. Was somebody there?

The senator disappeared around the corner, back toward the front door. Every blare of the car horn matched the increasing intensity of Reed's heartbeats. He fought to restore calm to his body, removing his finger from the trigger and rolling his head back until his neck popped. As the seconds ticked by, his urge to surrender to the tension grew. Reed wanted to smash the car and silence its incessant honking.

When Holiday reappeared in the kitchen, Reed

pressed his cheek against the stock and laid his finger back on the trigger. A quick twist of his arm pivoted the crosshairs from the living room back into the kitchen— back over the neck of his target. A second slipped by. He took half a breath. And then he saw her.

The breath froze in Reed's throat. He twisted the zoom to the 35x mark and stared through the glass. Her shoulder blades filled his view. Then her neck. Blonde waves fell over her shoulders, and long bangs were swept back over her ears, displaying just a shadow of rosy cheeks. Reed's hands were suddenly damp and swollen. He lifted his finger off the trigger and peeled his tongue from the roof of his mouth. His lips were dry, and his vision blurred around the woman as she turned toward him.

Banks.

The world stopped spinning, and he sat in trans-fixed stillness as the crosshairs hovered over her smile. She laughed and accepted a glass of wine from Holiday, and he gave her a side hug and kissed the top of her head. In the living room, they sat across from each other. Her long, elegant legs were crossed, revealing torn jeans and the white laces of her yellow sneakers.

The corners of his vision blurred. Each breath burned in his chest, burdening an already pounding heart. He pivoted the crosshairs back to Holiday, settled them over the base of his skull, and then touched the trigger.

One shot. I can't help it that she's here.

One breath. Two. He realigned with every blast of the car horn. The crosshairs twitched over his target, even though Holiday hadn't moved. Reed's breaths were shorter and more labored as he tightened his finger around the trigger . . . and then stopped. He shoved the rifle away from his shoulder and rolled onto his back, covering his face with both hands. "*Shit!*"

He lay on the roof. Whoever owned the SUV silenced the emergency alarm, and the parking lot fell quiet again. In the confused stillness that settled over him, nothing felt real. The world and every trained sense that he had honed in on this one shot only moments before were shattered. His focus, practiced calm, cold calculation—all of it was gone. All he could see was her face—the bright blue eyes, enchanting smile, the grace, and seduction of her every casual move. Each sensation tore through his mind more violently than his bullet would have ever torn through Holiday. They dominated him and reduced him to a numb and disoriented child.

Reed's hands shook as he disassembled the rifle, crammed the parts back into the bag, and jogged back to the ladder. The hangover headache from hours before returned as he dropped off the bottom rung, and every pound of his boots on the concrete echoed in his head with intensifying pain as he made his way back to the Camaro.

He dialed Brent.

"Yeah, boss?"

"Cancel the hit." Reed's voice snapped in the light breeze.

"Um, what?"

"The Holiday job. Cancel it. I'm out."

"Reed, whatever happened, just walk it off, okay? We can—"

"I said cancel it, dammit. This isn't a debate."

Brent was quiet for a moment. Reed slammed the Camaro's door shut and fumbled in the passenger seat for a bottle of water, but there was nothing except the empty Coke can from earlier that day.

"Reed, listen to me. As your broker. You're about to make a huge mistake. This is number thirty, right? You don't wanna back out on this one. It could send a really bad message."

Reed's shoulders tensed. "How did you know about that?"

"Enfield told me. He didn't get specific, he just said you were under contract for thirty hits. Some kind of private deal between the two of you."

Reed rubbed his chin, digging his fingers into his own skin until they went numb.

"I never intended to continue past thirty. Tell them to get me another target, and I'll finish the hit list, but I won't kill Holiday."

"That's something you can tell them yourself. I'm not getting in the middle of your contract. It's nothing personal, but I won't go down with you."

Reed felt fire flood his veins. "Are you serious?"

"You might be ready to flush your career, but I'm not. These people are serious, Reed. You made a commitment. If you walk out, we can't work together anymore."

"Fine. Nice knowing you." Reed threw the phone

into the passenger seat and slammed his open palm against the dash.

Why him? Why Banks? Just one shot away. Three pounds of pressure applied to a performance trigger—that was all that stood between him and the open highway.

What the hell have I done?

The Atlantic wasn't visible from where he was parked, but he could still see her face. It was forever burned into his memory. He'd never met a woman like Banks, and he didn't know why he felt this way, but there was no turning back now. Everything was on the line. He had to see her again.

10

North Georgia

L eather met leather with a wet thud. Sweat sprayed from the glove, showering the white bag in a blast of hot drops. Reed danced back on his right foot, shifting his weight over the ball of his left before lunging forward again.

Whoomp, whoomp. Each stroke jarred his shoulder. Sweat streamed into his eyes, further blurring his bloodshot vision. Another combo to the middle of the bag. Then a headlock. Two death kicks with his left shin. Another stroke on the side of the bag, just where the temple would be. Each blow fell faster than the last. The chain that suspended the bag creaked and jerked against the rafters, threatening to give way under the onslaught of enraged strokes. Reed danced back on his toes and drove a right cross, followed by a left hook, straight into the white leather. He breathed through his mouth between each blow. A hiss, and then a thud.

Always in that order. So close together, the sounds melded into an indistinguishable roar, like distant thunder masked by torrential rain beating down on a metal roof.

Shhh. Whoomp. Whoomp. Two distance-testing jabs. *Shhh. Whoomp.* A blow strong enough to crush bone.

Reed stumbled back, allowing his jaw to fall slack as he gasped for air. His bare chest glimmered, and the blood pounding through his veins sent waves of dizziness through his brain, only subjected to reason by larger waves of adrenaline. Power and chaos were always at war with each other for total control of his body.

The light bulb mounted on the cabin wall shone over the back porch. As the bag continued to swing and creek, Reed collapsed against the rail. The night wasn't warm—not for an October night—but after half an hour of incessant pounding, he would have sweated in a snowstorm.

"Baxter! Beer me." Reed peeled off the gloves and tossed them onto a nearby table.

The back door hung open. Toenails clicked against hardwood, followed by the scuffling, snorting sound of the bulldog sinking his teeth into the towrope attached to the refrigerator door. Rows of brown beer bottles were conveniently stowed in the lower door pocket, right at eye-level for the grouchy pooch. A few seconds passed, then Baxter appeared on the back porch with the neck of a beer bottle clamped between his yellow teeth. He dropped it on the rough-sawn decking of the porch, then snorted and sat down.

Reed took a moment to wipe thick streams of doggy saliva off the bottle before popping off the lid against the rail.

Cold and fizzy. The light beer stung his throat and erupted like explosive sandpaper against his tongue.

Reed waved the bottle at Baxter. "That's a good beer."

The bulldog raised one eyebrow at him, then snorted again.

"No. We've been over this. No beer for you. That's animal abuse. Do I look like a criminal to you?"

Baxter closed his eyes as though the effort of staring at the quiet trees around the cabin were just too much strain. His bottom teeth jutted out between his lips, gleaming with slobber under the faint light. In spite of his disgruntled appearance, Reed knew he was content. This was Baxter's favorite time of day.

Reed finished the beer, then flung the bottle at the punching bag. It bounced off and spun into the darkness, crashing into the leaves. Waves of tension rushed through his chest, causing his muscles to tighten.

I was so close. One shot. One trigger pull. It was almost over.

Oliver would call. The kingpin killer would demand answers. There was no excuse for backing out of a hit. It simply wasn't done. Oliver's contractors *always* delivered. It was the hallmark of his company—their core belief. Whatever happens. Whatever it takes. Finish the job.

"I don't have answers," Reed spoke between dry lips. The lie tasted stale as soon as it left his tongue. Obvious and cheap. Oh, he had answers. He knew exactly why he hadn't pulled the trigger, but it wasn't an answer he could offer Oliver.

Reed could hear him now—the words snapping off his tongue like darts full of venom. *You did* what?"

Reed stood up and placed his palms over the railing.

Does she love him? The thought snapped through his mind with all the explosive energy of an atom bomb. So clear and so obvious. *Does Banks love Holiday? Are they together? Does she smile and laugh with him the way she smiled and laughed on top of that parking garage?*

Each thought stung a little harder than the last. Reed slammed his closed fist into the railing, then drove his toe into the rough planks. Pain shot up his foot as blood dripped from a busted toenail.

What's wrong with me? Why do I care? Why didn't I just pull the damn trigger?

Once again, he saw her gliding across the kitchen, holding the wineglass between her delicate fingers. He saw the way her socks twisted when she spun over the expensive tile, and the flash in her eyes when she hugged Holiday. Was that love? Was that *love* in her eyes?

Reed shouted and drove another punch into the rail, then glared at Baxter. The dog lifted his head and stared up at Reed with concern and uncertainty.

"Three years. Three years I've been working this job. One trigger pull away from the end, and I flip out over some damn girl? No, don't worry. I'll get it done. There's over twenty hours left. It's just the jitters . . . we've seen this before."

Reed paced the porch, running his fingers through his dripping hair. Each footfall echoed in his tired brain like the roll of a drum, regulating his breathing and helping him to focus. He couldn't return to the Ikea. There was too much risk in appearing there for a third time. He needed a new strategy—another place to strike Holiday. There was still time to formulate a secondary plan, but first, he would need to rest.

Oliver wouldn't call as long as there was still time on the kill clock. Those precious hours could be leveraged to clean this mess up, complete the job, collect the paycheck, and pack up shop—just like he planned. He'd drive far, far away from bloody Atlanta and all the bad memories it contained.

Banks's beautiful face crossed his mind and derailed his train of thought, sending it careening down a new path in the time it took him to blink. Her laugh, so bright and happy, was enough to light the darkest corner of Hell.

She feels like home.

The thought shattered the cloud of confusion around his mind as though it were made of ice. *She feels like home.* He thought again about the house at the foot of the mountains. The rocking chair on the front porch. Banks scratching Baxter behind the ears.

Home is the one thing I've never had. The only thing I want when this carnage is finally over.

Reed jerked the phone out of his pocket and dialed.

"Winter."

"Why didn't you tell me about her relationship with Holiday?" Reed shot off the question before Winter had a chance to draw a breath.

"Excuse me?"

"Senator Holiday." Reed smacked his palm against the railing. "You didn't tell me they were involved."

The line was silent. Reed didn't know if he had caught Winter off guard, or if Winter was simply giving him time to stop shouting.

"First of all"—Winter spoke in a measured monotone—"they aren't involved. He's her godfather. And second, this information was notated on page six of the report. Perhaps you didn't read the entire file."

Reed's mind spun, and he blinked through tired eyes. "Godfather? What the hell are you talking about?"

Winter paused again. Now Reed was almost sure the delay was meant to rebuke him.

"Senator Holiday was close friends with Miss Morccelli's father. They were frat brothers at Vanderbilt. The details are in the file."

Reed lowered the phone and stared into the trees, reviewing the memories one at a time. The way Holiday smiled when she entered the room, how he hugged her from the side, and kissed her on the head. His casual demeanor as he handed her the wine.

No. They weren't together, but they were clearly close—in a father-daughter way. Or, in this case, a godfather way. Holiday was a safe place for Banks—a kind, loyal friend.

And I was going to kill him.

Reed jammed the phone against his ear. "Who ordered the hit?" Once again, silence hung on the line, but this time Reed wasn't having it.

"I know you know. Who ordered the hit?"

"This is thirty, isn't it?"

The sudden question sent an icy chill down Reed's spine. He pressed the phone against his cheek and wrapped his fingers around the railing.

"*What*?"

"This is your thirtieth kill. They call it the freedom bell."

"How the hell do you know that?"

"I've contracted with Oliver Enfield's company for a long time, Reed. I've seen a lot of good contractors come ... *and* go."

Tension shot down his arms as he dug his fingers into the wood. "What does that mean?"

Winter didn't answer. The silence was so thick, Reed felt as though Winter was sitting beside him.

"Who ordered the hit?" he shouted into the phone.

When Winter replied, the monotone was gone and replaced with a hint of menace.

"Watch your back, Reed. Freedom has a nasty bite."

The line clicked off. Reed's hands shook as he pried the phone away from his ear and stared at the blank screen. Winter had never broken character before and never expressed interest in him as a killer.

Winter had never expressed a warning.

The breach in behavior sent a sting ripping down Reed's back—an army of fire ants digging into his skin.

Who ordered the hit?

Reed snapped his fingers at Baxter and walked back into the house. Everything about this contract felt different and wrong. A voice in the back of his head whispered at him between the blasts of noise and chaos, and he couldn't discern the words, but he heard the voice, muffled and confused.

Mitchell Holiday might well deserve to die, but Reed wasn't taking the shot until he knew why. Nobody forced him into a corner, and nobody could make him take away this woman's godfather without knowing why. It was time to jerk back the curtain and find some answers.

He would start with Banks.

11

Decatur, Georgia

Glistening globes of dew still clung to each blade of browned grass, even as the sun arced toward its noon-time high, bathing Decatur in welcome warmth. The cough-rumble of the Camaro felt as blasphemous to the peace of the morning as a raunchy laugh in a graveyard, and Reed switched the car off and sat in silence as he surveyed the duplex, tired and old with peeling paint. Bits of sunbaked shingles lay in the flowerbed at random. Plastic jack-o'-lanterns guarded the entrance, their crooked smiles leering at Reed as if they knew why he had come, but they just didn't give a damn. A stray tabby cat bounced across the porch and around the house, chasing a butterfly between the bushes. But there were no people, no laughing children or bustling adults. The neighborhood, which consisted entirely of battered duplexes and brick apartment homes, was as cold and unfriendly as a warzone—decay and despair, and too little of everything.

A couple of teenagers wandered out of a side street, bouncing a basketball and talking in subdued mumbles. Reed waited for them to pass within easy earshot of the car, then he whistled. "Hey. You guys know a blonde girl who lives here?"

They stopped and stared at him as though he were an invader, armed to the teeth and ready to burn down what was left of their battered homes.

So then, Banks wasn't home. A twinge of defeat bubbled in his stomach, or was it just disappointment? Maybe he should go back to Atlanta and check the nightclub. But it didn't open until late afternoon, and anyway, if Banks left home to run errands, she would most likely do that locally. One of the numerous grocery stores or farmer's markets in the area were likely destinations for a morning shopping trip.

It was a good bet. He spotted the yellow Volkswagen fifteen minutes later, parked in front of her bank. He left the Camaro a hundred yards away in an adjoining supermarket lot and jogged toward the squat brick building. He wasn't sure what his plan was. Maybe he would pretend he was at the bank on personal business. Make it out to be a coincidence. Then ask her out to lunch and talk to her. Find out about Holiday. Figure out what the hell was going on.

His thoughts trailed off as he passed the Beetle. He stopped and stared at the rusty antique, remembering the clatter of the underpowered engine—the squeak of the suspension at every turn. The way Banks drove with reckless abandon—as though she were the only person on the road—the perpetual smile on her face, and the way the wind tossed her hair.

The front door of the bank slammed shut as a customer walked out. Reed looked back at the Beetle, then walked toward the door.

The bank was cold and sterile, and gaudy marketing covered the walls. Glass offices lined the perimeter of a crowded waiting area. A line of a dozen impatient customers stood in front of the counter, and the tellers looked distant and detached, as though they were present in body alone. It was such a stark contrast to the five-star banking experience Reed was accustomed to through Lasquo Financial. The building was more like a title loan office than a bank.

"I don't know where it came from. It's not my money. That's the problem!"

Reed immediately recognized the thick Southern accent laden with emotion and frustration. Banks, with her back turned toward him, sat in one of the glass offices to his right. An overweight man with a thinning hairline and cheap glasses sat behind the desk, a look of exhaustion covering his chalky features.

"Ma'am, I realize you're upset. If you calm down, I'm sure we can figure this out."

"There's nothing to figure out. There's twenty-five thousand dollars in my account that doesn't belong to me. Take it out, please."

"Um, well, it's not that simple."

Banks rubbed her temples. "Why not?"

"Well, first of all, that would leave you overdrawn.

You were overdrawn when the wire posted to your account."

"I'm aware of that. I'll pay you in a couple days. It's been a rough week, okay? In the meantime, take the money out of my account. You guys should be more careful where you stick money."

The banker looked ready to shoot himself. "Ma'am, I already told you. We don't 'stick money' in people's accounts. The wire was made payable directly to you, with your account number notated. We credited it to your account accordingly."

"Well, I don't want it!" Banks smacked the desk with her palm.

The banker sat forward, rubbing his eyes with a shaky right hand.

"Miss Morccelli, it's unfathomable to me that a person in your position would be so opposed—"

"My position? And just *what is* my position, exactly?" A tinge of indignation edged into her voice.

The banker backpedaled. "That's not what I meant. I'm just saying—"

"That I'm a broke-ass overdrafter? That's it. Close my account. I'm not dealing with this. I don't need anybody's help!"

Reed stood still by the door, transfixed by the scene unfolding in front of him. He wasn't sure how he expected Banks to respond when twenty-five grand appeared in her account out of nowhere. Stupidly, he assumed she would be grateful and apply the windfall toward her medical debt. He now realized how arrogant and belittling that assumption had been, but he was still taken aback by her vehement refusal to accept or even entertain a handout. It was fiercely independent. Aggressively proud.

Ridiculously attractive.

An annoyed voice grabbed his attention.

"Can I help you, sir?" A short woman wearing a crooked name badge leered at him. She looked utterly done with life.

Reed realized he was standing in the middle of the lobby with his hands in his pockets. "No. I'm good," he said as he rushed back outside.

He was a fool for assuming Banks would simply take the money. More than that, he was an asshole for tracking her down. She was independent and didn't want to be babied, which explained why she was the goddaughter of a millionaire and still drove a rattle-trap of a car and was in debt up to her ears. She didn't want the help. She had it covered. More than that, she didn't have time to fix his problems. Holiday was his problem, and roping Banks into the middle of this mess wouldn't be fair to her. He would have to find the answers he needed without exposing her to whatever menace ordered the hit.

Before he could start the engine of the Camaro, his phone vibrated in his pocket. The dark screen read "UNKNOWN."

Reed hesitated, then hit the answer button and said nothing while he waited for the caller to speak first.

"You screwed up, Montgomery." The voice was computerized, like that of an automated answering machine.

"Who is this?"

"Somebody who doesn't like being let down, Reed. Somebody who feels very let down by your failure to assassinate Senator Holiday."

A rush of warmth flooded Reed's cheeks, and his heart rate accelerated. The sounds and distractions of the supermarket parking lot vanished around him.

"Look, smartass. I never fail, and I don't deal with anyone over the phone. You got a problem, call my broker."

"I'm afraid your broker is quite indisposed at the moment."

"What?"

Reed's voice was drowned out by a blood-curdling scream. Agony flooded the phone, echoing as though it came from an amphitheater. Reed jerked the phone away from his ear as he caught his breath. The screams continued, ringing as though they were voiced straight from Hell. Pleas for mercy were mixed with dull groans and shrill shrieks, all fused into one horrific chorus.

The air inside the Camaro was suddenly thick and sticky, as though Reed were breathing through a straw. He held the phone against his knee, muting the hellish voice of death. Moments felt like hours, until at last the screams faded, and the computerized tone took over.

"I sent you pictures. You have twelve hours to finish the job. Don't test me."

Reed swallowed back the dryness in his mouth and punched the steering wheel. Before he could respond, the caller hung up, leaving the screen vacant. A moment later, the first text appeared. Reed's fingers felt thick and heavy as he unlocked his phone. The ghastly image that greeted him sent waves of nausea ripping through his stomach.

Brent.

He lay on a concrete floor, tied between wooden posts, his face twisted into a death scream. Shreds of skin and flesh decorated the floor beside him, exposing an empty stomach cavity. He was disemboweled, gutted from throat to groin.

Blinding rage replaced nausea, and Reed jammed the car into gear and dumped the clutch. The rear tires screamed against the pavement, screeching over the howl of the engine as the rear end of the vehicle swung outward. The rubber caught, and the Camaro rocketed forward out of the parking lot and back onto the highway.

Back toward Atlanta.

12

"I need you to post a hit for me," Reed shouted over the thunder of the engine. The fall breeze snapped around the mirrors and battered the headliner of the car, stinging his eyes. The wind tasted fresh and clean—a welcome relief against the smothering feeling against his chest.

Nobody answered, and Reed rolled up the windows. "Winter, did you hear me?"

A dry voice coughed, then Winter's stagnant tone flowed from the speaker.

"Who is the target?"

"Senator Mitchell Holiday."

This time the pause felt heavy, as though it were laden with unspoken thoughts and conflicting emotions. Reed didn't have time for either.

"Did you hear me? Can you do it or not?"

Another dry cough. "What's the bounty?"

"I don't care. Half a million."

Reed thought he heard the scratch of a pen on

paper, but maybe it was just the squeak of whatever robotic entity Winter consisted of.

"My service fee is twenty-five hundred. I'll draft your account. Any special requests?"

"Yes. I want it posted to Section 13, dark web."

The pen tapped on the notepad. Reed could hear each slow click.

"Are you aware that Section 13 has been compromised by the FBI?"

"I am. Post it anonymously. Ignore anyone who's dumb enough to respond."

"Very well. The listing will be live in twenty minutes."

Nausea returned to the pit of Reed's stomach, boiling like a jar of sour vegetable oil. Every muscle in his body was tense. He downshifted into fourth and blew past a semi-truck. The nervousness growing in the back of his mind washed over him in waves—it was something a little worse than shock, and a little less than panic.

Brent was dead—slaughtered like a pig. It was a blatant attack on his own doorstep by a defiant challenger. Nothing like this had ever happened before. Reed wasn't particularly attached to Brent, or to anyone he worked with, but Brent was the partner he spoke to most often. He knew Brent had blond hair and loved mint ice cream and video games. The chatty broker was from Detroit and had a mother he sent checks to every month in a nursing home. She thought he worked for a military history museum in Rome. She had no idea her son was neck-deep in the mire of organized crime, and she would never know what fate befell him. He would simply vanish, gone without a trace, snuffed out like any one of Reed's victims.

The thought brought renewed rage into Reed's soul. No, he didn't care about Brent, not personally, but a line had been crossed. A line that couldn't be ignored. The contract had now spilled far, far beyond the realms of acceptable business practices, even for the criminal underworld. There was a debt to pay and a statement to make.

You don't shit on Reed Montgomery's doorstep and walk away breathing.

Reed snatched up his phone and speed-dialed the first contact, focusing on calming his nerves and backing away from a precipice of uncontrolled, rampaging madness. The answering machine picked up and greeted him with a single-word message: "Enfield." Then the beep.

"Oliver." The word snapped like a gunshot, and Reed forced himself to take another breath before continuing. "We need to talk immediately. Call me back as soon as you get this."

Reed rolled the windows down again and sucked in a lungful of air, which helped restore control over his body. He checked the clock on the dash and counted backward to the phone call with Winter.

He'd give it another hour, and then he would cancel the hit.

13

Senator Mitchell Holiday, known to his friends and foes alike as "Fighting Mitch," was feeling the wear of civil service. He sat behind the broad oak desk in his congressional office and set his reading glasses on the table. His back hurt. His neck hurt. He had a headache. And his damn knee was acting up again.

The plush leather of his office chair squeaked as Holiday leaned back. He didn't drink at the office—not anymore, anyway—but a bourbon, smooth and strong, would've really taken the edge off. He laid his hands on the arms of the chair and sat perfectly still, letting the stress and strain seep out of him.

His knee burned like fire, and he straightened his leg, attempting to relieve the strain. It was an old football injury. Holiday played for Grand Republic Preparatory School in Savannah as a running back. That was where Fighting Mitch was born. Given a chance, he always chose to run the ball straight through the defensive line instead of around. He was a sensation. Local sports commentators called him NFL talent, the pride of South Georgia. Right up to the moment the two-hundred-eighty-pound senior from Athens crashed into his shoulder and slammed him to the ground, leaving his foot caught in the soft mud. When his knee exploded, it snuffed out all ambitions of a football career in a split second.

Grand Republic was losing that night. Down twenty-one points with an Athens quarterback who had their number. But when Holiday hit the mud, vengeful fire that could've won them a Super Bowl erupted through his team. He could still hear his quarterback, Danny McKnight, shouting at the offensive line moments before the snap. He could see the explosion of glistening rainwater as shoulder pads and helmets crashed together. And then, with only seconds left on the clock, he could hear the roar of the crowd as the ball flipped between the uprights. It was the biggest upset of the season.

Holiday would never forget that night. He refused medical care until the end of the game, at which point his teammates carried him off the field on their shoulders as Danny screamed and threw his helmet into the air. Grand Republic's quarterback went on to serve in the National Guard, deployed for Desert Storm, where he was blown in half by a landmine. Holiday wasn't there, but he heard that blast in his nightmares. He imagined Danny lying in the mud, his blue eyes wide and empty, as if to say, "Where are you, Mitch? Why aren't you here to carry me off the field?"

Real life was so much colder than football. Upsets were never as simple as a field goal.

The chair groaned again as Holiday sat up. He lifted a cigarette from the desk drawer and flicked his thumb against a polished Zippo lighter. Icy waves of menthol filled his lungs, loosening his muscles and easing the tension on his strained nerves. He leaned back and dragged another cloud of smoke from the cigarette. It burned and soothed all at the same time. In the temporary relaxation of the nicotine, he could still see Danny pumping his fist in the air and grinning at the crowd. Today, in this moment, Holiday didn't feel much like Fighting Mitch anymore. He'd give anything to have Danny here, to have the whole team carry him out of the chaotic hell he called home.

Holiday walked to the window and gazed out of the Georgia State Capitol and over the busy streets of downtown Atlanta. If he survived the remainder of the term, he would sell the logistics company. Sell the house in Brunswick, the condo here in Atlanta, and the cabin in North Carolina. Leave an inheritance for Banks and disappear out west somewhere. He'd always wanted to live out west. Holiday was a wealthy man, and for all his grandeur and resources, Georgia had chained him down his entire life. Maybe he could finally cut loose and buy a cabin someplace in the mountains of Wyoming, miles and miles from anyone and everyone. Get a dog and name him Burt, for no reason at all. Drive an old, beat-up pickup truck and hunt in the summer. Write a book in the winter. He'd always wanted to try his hand at a novel, but he just never had the time.

A trail of scarlet embers rained through the air as Holiday flicked the cigarette into a brass trash can. He rubbed his eyes with both hands, then jammed his thumb against the speaker button on his desk phone.

"Yes, sir?"

"Get me Matt Rollick."

As the smoke faded from his lungs, Holiday could already feel his chest begin to tighten again. The air in the big office was thick and hot, as though he were sitting in a sauna. He picked up a pen and clicked it. Open. Closed. Open again. Each snap of the pen was a small explosion in the still room. His fingers stuck against the cheap plastic, leaving smudges on the barrel.

"Agent Rollick." The voice, loud and jarring, crackled over the speakerphone.

Holiday switched to the receiver.

"This is Senator Holiday. I'm calling you in reference to our conversation yesterday."

After a rustle of papers from the other end of the line, Rollick's voice softened some, but he remained all-business.

"Glad to hear from you, Senator. Where do we stand regarding the FBI's offer?"

Open. Closed. The pen clicked again, and Holiday stared at the writing on its barrel. Some local pest control company. God only knew how it found its way to his desk. He ran his tongue across dry lips, then set the pen down.

"I need assurances regarding my goddaughter."

"Banks?"

"Yes. I want her left out of this. Completely. No interviews. No media. No agency attention. Nothing."

"You know I can't guarantee that, Senator."

"Then you don't have a deal. I'll burn in Hell before I watch her dragged through this mess."

"If you don't cooperate, you may very well get your wish. I can commit to distance from the agency, assuming you give us everything we need to know. I have no control over the media."

"No good, agent. I've made it clear from day one that Banks will not be involved."

"She isn't involved. I don't see the problem."

"It's her father. I want the agency's commitment that they won't turn this into a smear campaign, and that the media will be left out of it."

"I'm not in charge of media relations. I'm an investigator. My job is to investigate. If you're not willing to cooperate, you may be facing media attention of your own. Your hands aren't clean, Senator. Don't forget that."

"Are you threatening me?"

"I'm reminding you of the cards you've been dealt. This could be your last chance to step out of this alive. When this investigation sees the light of day, I won't be able to protect you if you're not on my side. Do you understand what I'm saying, Senator?"

The room was suddenly calm as if the world were holding its breath. Holiday sucked in the thick and stale air and tapped his finger against the desktop.

His mind raced, but really, there wasn't much to decide.

"Banks is given protective custody. Complete isolation from the media. And Frank is a hero. Do you hear me? No smearing. The man died a hero."

Rollick sighed. "I'm not going to make promises I can't keep. You either trust me or you don't. There are no guarantees."

"Then there's no deal. Good luck unraveling this cluster on your own."

Holiday slammed the headset back onto the hook and clenched his fist. Exhaustion overwhelmed his mind. It was the sort of total, crushing fatigue that no amount of rest or nicotine could relieve. It was death itself knocking at his doorstep.

He sat in perfect stillness for what must have been half an hour. Rollick would call back. The investigator couldn't drop a witness this crucial. He would make some calls and find a way to meet Holiday's demands. And then he would call back.

Holiday suddenly wondered if God was listening. He hadn't prayed in twenty years. Not since his high school sweetheart and the love of his life, Mary Truant Anderson, wasted away on an Atlanta hospital bed, eaten alive by what should have been a curable cancer. None of the medications had any effect, and none of the treatments slowed it down. It devoured her body in a matter of weeks, draining her away to a mere shadow of her old self before the life breath finally left her lungs.

It was as though God himself had sucked the life

out of her and struck her down right in the prime of life, for no reason or purpose. She was a beautiful soul. A loving, kind-hearted angel. Somebody who truly didn't deserve to die.

If God wouldn't listen to prayers for somebody as beautiful as Mary, there was no way he would hear prayers for somebody as battered and war-torn as Mitchell Holiday. There was blood on these hands.

The intercom buzzed, jarring Holiday back to the present.

"Senator, there's men here from the FBI. They want . . . Wait! You can't go in there!"

The door slammed back on its hinges, crashing into the mahogany wall with a thunderclap. Holiday jumped up and shoved the chair in front of him, his fight-or-flight instincts kicking in with a wave of panic. Four men wearing black suits and stern glares barged through the door. The lead guy flashed a gold badge and stomped right up to the desk.

"Agent Wes Harper, FBI. You need to come with us, Senator."

Holiday clutched the back of his chair, and his knuckles turned white. He took a slow breath and forced himself to assume the diplomatic confidence that won his elections. Calm. Southern. Just a little indignant. "Agent, you can't just bust in here. I've already told Agent Rollick I'm not going anywhere until my demands are met. That's the final word on this matter."

Harper's brow wrinkled. The hand holding the

badge fell to his side, and he turned to one of his colleagues, who only shrugged.

Holiday swallowed, feeling his stomach twist into a knot. The moments ticked by in slow motion.

Harper turned back. He shoved the badge into his pocket and stepped to the side, motioning to the door. "I have no idea what you're talking about, Senator, but you need to come with us. There's been a credible threat to your life. You are now under the protective custody of the FBI."

14

The fall wind blowing off the mountains brought a bite with it when Reed stepped out of the Camaro. Leaves rattled across the gravel driveway and tumbled over one another, and the chill penetrated his jacket, sending a slight shiver down his back. He shoved his hands deeper into his pockets and kicked at the steps of the porch, knocking dirt off his shoes. Baxter lay just inside the door, snoring like a troll with a lake of drool gathering around his snout. Reed knelt beside him and scratched behind his floppy ears. Baxter's snores became more regular, and his body fell limp under the gentle stroking.

There was something singularly peaceful about a sleeping dog. Reed often found himself envying the simple life of his pet, and he couldn't help but smile as he thought how far the fat pooch had come from the mangy stray that showed up on his doorstep two years before. That dog had been only days from death, and more than a little gun shy of humanity. But as the weeks passed, a strange connection developed between them. Maybe they were both beat-up and scarred and scared of the world. Maybe they both needed a friend who didn't ask too many questions.

The gas stove hissed and clicked as Reed flipped it on then set a skillet over the flame. He dropped a thick ribeye into the pan and was rewarded by the sizzle of red meat frying on hot iron. The little cabin was flooded with the greasy aroma of quality beef, followed by the sound of Baxter rolling to his feet and wobbling into the kitchen.

"Nice nap?" Reed flipped the steak and sprinkled seasoning from an unmarked bottle over the browned side. Baxter snorted and sat down beside him, panting and staring at the pan.

"There's been a problem," Reed muttered. "Somebody took a dump on our front porch. Gonna have to do something about it."

Grease sizzled and spat from the pan. Reed flipped the steak onto a plate and then dumped a can of green beans into a saucepan before setting it on the stove. Soon the water began to bubble and steam as the beans danced beneath the rolling surface.

"The thing is . . . there's this girl. I met her the other night, and I was gonna tell you about her. I don't know, man. She's something else."

Reed opened a can of dog food and kicked Baxter's bowl out from under the cabinet before dumping the slop into it. Baxter snorted and looked at the steak.

"You ever met a girl—or dog—who just made the world go 'round? You know. Maybe a French bulldog. I could see you with a Frenchie."

Water bubbled over the edge of the pan. Reed lifted it off the stove and dumped the water into the sink before emptying the beans onto the plate. An icy cold German lager from the fridge completed the menu. Reed sat at the table and wiped the grease off a fork and knife from his dinner the night before. The first bite of steak tasted perfect. Tender and red, with just a trace of blood oozing from the center.

"I don't know, man. Right now, there are more pressing issues. Somebody took out Brent, and I'm not sure what to do about it. What would you do?"

Baxter sat beside the table with his head tilted to one side, and his lower teeth jutting out over his lip. Drool dripped down the side of his face. Reed cut a piece of ribeye from the edge of the steak and dropped it over his nose. Baxter wolfed it down in one swallow and returned to his previous pose.

Reed took a bite of green beans and waved his fork at the dog. "This is my steak. You want steak, you get a job. I've had about enough of your freeloading. You don't even sweep the damn porch."

The old bulldog woofed spit over Reed's leg then wandered back into the kitchen and contented himself with slurping up the bowl of dog food. Reed pulled the phone out of his pocket. He tried calling Oliver, and once more was sent to voicemail. It was unlike his boss to not answer, and even more out of character for him to not call back.

Oliver remained highly connected to his organization. Even though his contractors operated with a certain level of anonymity, Oliver kept close tabs on their activities and needs. His unexpected distance was disconcerting.

The last bite of steak, washed down with a swallow of beer, made a perfect finale to a delicious meal. Reed set the plate on the floor for Baxter to lick clean, then relocated to his desk and powered on the laptop. He needed to learn everything he could about Mitchell Holiday. Usually, he would short-circuit the research project and assign the job to Winter, but Reed was starting to feel unsure about the ghost, who typically made it a practice to remain detached and neutral in all business dealings. Winter's cryptic warning from the night before left Reed feeling more than a little uneasy.

Google would have to take Winter's place for now. A quick search produced a handful of old blogs, social media posts, and even pictures of Holiday in grade school. An article from a Savannah newspaper detailed Holiday's tragic football injury and how it derailed multiple collegiate scholarships. A few sources mentioned legislative actions and business dealings, but nothing was very helpful. By all accounts, Holiday was a traditional, low-level politician, hallmarked by occasional controversy and a handful of red-letter moments. Nothing special. Certainly nothing worth killing a man over.

Whatever Holiday had stumbled into, it wasn't a public matter, and that wasn't surprising. Reed's contracts usually involved underhanded deals gone bad.

By now, the FBI would have red-flagged the hit listing on the dark web and placed Holiday under protective custody, probably in one of the Capitol Police buildings downtown. Reed appreciated the breathing room that provided him, but he knew it wouldn't last. Whoever killed Brent had already demonstrated vicious intolerance for being defied, and placing Holiday under the nose of the FBI was far from checkmate.

"They'll come after me next," he said aloud. "A dominance kill. Probably back off on Holiday for a bit. Wait for things to cool down."

And then I'm going to burn their party down. His thought wasn't an emotional decision—just an inevitable one. When this was done—when the smoke settled and he checked off the thirtieth kill and disappeared forever—he couldn't leave any loose ends behind.

The last drops of beer tasted warm and bitter. Reed tossed the bottle into the trash, stood up, popped his neck, and started toward the bathroom.

The phone rang.

Reed pried it out of his pocket, feeling his stomach tighten. Only one word illuminated the screen: "UNKNOWN."

He hit the green button, and didn't wait for the computerized voice to speak first.

"All right, jerk-off. Now he's under protective custody. Your turn to listen."

The speaker echoed with a hissing sound—slow breaths from a dry throat. To Reed's surprise, the voice wasn't computerized. The tone was calm and icy cold. A hint of a South American accent dampened each word. Venezuelan, maybe. Or Colombian.

"You're clever, aren't you?"

A cold sweat ran down Reed's neck. He leaned over the table and dug his fingernails into the wood. "Who the hell is this?"

"You can call me Salvador. I'm the man who resents being toyed with. You're toying with me, Reed."

The derision in the voice was as thick and heavy as the tone was sharp.

Reed balled his fingers into a fist and slammed them into the table.

"You think I'm toying with you? Well, let me clue you in on our next playdate. I'm going to rip your face off, one bloody strip at a time. By the time I'm finished, you—"

A shriek broke the silence. "Stop! Back off!"

Reed's palms went cold. He knew that voice. How could he ever forget it?

Banks.

"Do I have your attention, Reed?" The speaker was still calm, but Reed could hear the impatience in his tone.

"What are you doing?" Reed hissed.

"I think you know. I have Miss Morccelli. You know Miss Morccelli, don't you? Two nights ago, you sat on the edge of the parking garage at Lindbergh Station while she played the ukulele. It was a beautiful song. I still have a copy of the recording if you're interested."

Bile welled up in Reed's throat, tasting both acidic and bitter at the same time. It was all he could do not to scream. He felt his windpipe closing, and he focused all of his energy on controlling his response.

"What do you want?"

"The same thing I've always wanted. I want you to kill Mitchell Holiday. It's going to be a lot harder now, thanks to your little stunt with the dark web. But that's your problem. You'll find him on the fourth floor of an FBI field office at the corner of 5th and Washington. It's an unmarked support office. Blow up the whole building if you want. Just get it done. You have until sundown. Every fifteen minutes after dark, I'm going to cut off one of Banks's fingers. If she runs out of fingers, I'm going to begin filleting her from the neck down. That sounds deadly, but it's not. It could take hours for her to bleed out, and I won't be in a hurry. Do you understand me, Reed?"

The cabin fell silent, and a chill filled Reed's soul. He closed his eyes and focused on each breath, each muscle movement. The dark clouds in his head began to dissipate, and his fighting instincts and the cold calculation of a natural killer took over.

"I need assurances that she won't be harmed before sundown."

"You have them. But this is your last chance. Finish the job."

15

Light flooded the basement and dust hung in the air as Reed pounded down the stairs and walked straight to the gun safe. His hands were damp and numb as he spun the dial three times to clear it, then entered the combination and twisted the bolt handle. Fire and a blinding rush of something between rage and hatred flooded his veins. He reached into the safe and pulled out a KRISS Vector submachine gun chambered in .45 ACP.

One thing rang perfectly clear through his muddled mind: He could not think about Banks. It was all he could do to push the sound of her agonized screams out of his mind and focus on the task at hand, but he knew if he didn't try, the rage would overwhelm him.

Rage puts you in the fast lane to dying hard. Oliver said it a thousand times.

Reed set the gun on the table. With only four hours until sunset, there was no time to strategize or create a subtle plan of attack. He had only one option—kick down the door, clear the room, and find Mitch Holiday. The senator was his best bet of finding Banks.

Reed peeled off his sweat-drenched jeans before retrieving a pair of cargo pants pre-strung with a heavy leather belt. A black T-shirt, black boots, and a set of body armor plates completed his outfit, masking his frame into the classic picture of an American killer. He checked the straps of the body armor and cinched them down further until it hurt to breathe. His chest was already tight, and his mind numb. Every action was practiced and mechanical. There was no time to think.

Reed returned to the safe and selected a drop leg holster. He strapped it to his right thigh before sliding a loaded and chambered Glock 31 pistol inside. Another belt holding two full pistol mags, a Ka-Bar knife, and a flashlight went over his gun belt. Next came the chest rig, loaded with six submachine gun magazines, each filled with lead-nose cartridges. Above the magazines, Reed clipped three flashbangs and a smoke grenade to the chest rig.

A sudden rush of blood fell from Reed's head, leaving a wave of dizziness behind it. He grabbed a shelf to steady himself, and for a moment focused on catching his breath.

They took her. And it's my fault.

Reed shook his head, forcing the thoughts out of his mind.

Go in cold, come out cold. Emotion is for suicidal assassins.

The heft of the KRISS Vector felt good under his calloused hands. Reed ran up the stairs and walked past a sleeping Baxter as he approached the front door.

"Don't wait up."

The roar of passing cars echoed through a supermarket parking lot three miles north of town, situated right next to the highway. Reed parked at the edge of the lot and carried his gear toward a silver SUV a few yards away. The Camaro was too impractical for the mission at hand, and he didn't want to risk having the plates photographed. The Toyota that sat by itself next to a shopping cart corral sported political stickers and the words "wash me" written in greasy finger smears over the back glass. It was a few years old, with a peeling clear coat and a cracked front bumper.

Reed set the bags down beside the SUV and dug into the pocket of his cargo pants. He produced a folding slim-jim and slid it between the glass and the water seal of the driver's window. A few minutes of careful manipulation with the tool were rewarded by the click of the lock. Reed opened the door and tossed his gun inside, then piled into the driver seat. The SUV was cluttered with fast-food wrappers, empty soda cans, and sales brochures for some real estate company. The stale stench of week-old French fries and sour cheese hung in the air like the ghost of drive-thru past, making him cough and wrinkle his nose. Reed tried to ignore the smell and dug beneath the steering column. He flipped a knife out of his pocket and worked for a couple more minutes before the starter clicked, and the engine whined to life.

As Reed put the car into drive, the congealed remains of some food byproduct stuck to his hands. He wiped his palms against his pants and piloted out of the lot and back onto the highway. Cars flashed past as he accelerated into the fast lane and drove toward the east side of Atlanta. Orange lights blanketed the city as the sun began its westward journey toward the ends of the earth. The knots in his stomach tightened, and he rolled the windows down.

Banks was alone. Afraid. Hurting. They had tortured her. He saw those big blue eyes again—so wide and deep—and he imagined them full of fear. Was it worse to know she was in pain, or worse to know he couldn't do anything to stop it?

In cold. Out cold. Clear your head, Reed.

He took the exit onto I-285 and pressed the accelerator deeper into the floor. The Toyota had half a tank of gas. He would get to the field office, take a few minutes to survey the situation, and then pull the trigger. There weren't a lot of options. He needed Holiday alive—at least for now. Unless and until the status quo changed, Reed wanted the senator as insurance, and possibly as a source of intel.

Why is Holiday still with the FBI? Why didn't they turn him over to Capitol Police?

The FBI building on the corner of Washington and

5th wasn't the bureau's primary facility for the city. Their official field office sat on Flowers Street, with a big lobby and an army of agents. He figured this building must be an off-grid secondary location used for more subtle operations. Did that mean the FBI knew why Holiday was wanted dead? Did Holiday have connections in the bureau?

No possible answer was a good one.

Anger and frustration boiled in Reed's veins as he approached the field office. He was cornered and forced into a hand of cards he didn't want to play. From the moment he accepted this damnable hit, everything had spun out of control. He was a puppet on a string, being jerked around and dragged toward an inevitable demise.

It would end today. He would recover Holiday, then retreat to a safe house. Sit down with the senator. Get to the bottom of this entire mess. Then negotiate for Banks's safe release. There would be time for vengeance later.

Reed parked the SUV in an alleyway between a gas station and a shopping strip, one block from the field office. After he cut the engine off, he sat in silence and surveyed his limited view of the street at the end of the alley. He couldn't see the field office. He hoped they couldn't see him.

What are you going to do, Reed? Storm the building, snatch him up, and haul ass? That's a horrible plan. You'll be gunned down.

Oliver's commanding voice echoed in the back of

his mind, a lesson the hardened killer had pounded into Reed's skull from day one: *Always be ready to walk away.*

The steering wheel was rock-hard under his grip, and his knuckles were white. He let go and rubbed his numb fingers. Oliver was right—the only course of action that ended in his favor was to walk away, torch the cabin, cash out some savings. Steal a car and go to ground—Mexico, maybe—and fade off the map. Vanish like the ghost he was.

He gritted his teeth. Why couldn't he walk away? He wasn't a hero, and he wasn't interested in becoming one. He made his living by pulling triggers and snapping necks. He never asked why, and he never harbored regrets. A man in his shoes didn't need honor, and he sure as hell didn't need a conscience. All he wanted was to be finished. To wash his hands and disappear forever.

Reed reached for the ignition wires. Their bare copper tips gleamed in the sunlight, promising freedom and security—everything he treasured and clung to.

Then he heard it faintly in the back of his mind, like the muted melody of an orchestra playing on the other side of a brick wall. It was the soft strumming of her ukulele. The enchanting murmur of her sweet voice, just above a whisper, singing to the Atlanta skyline. In an instant, every desperate, prehistoric impulse ignited within his body. The memory of her intoxicating smile. The touch of her lips on his.

The way she felt like home.

Reed slung the gun's harness over his neck and slammed the door shut, then reached into his cargo pocket and jerked out a three-hole ski mask. He pulled it over his head and checked his wristwatch. Two hours until sunset.

16

G lass shattered under Reed's boot as he kicked the door open and raised the gun. The receptionist didn't scream. She stood, stepped back, and reached for her handgun. Reed pulled the trigger twice. The bark of the submachine gun was deafening, and the bullets slammed into the wall just inches from the woman's ear. She blinked and stumbled, fumbling with the retention strap on her holster. Reed raced across the lobby and grabbed her by the back of the head, slamming her face into the desk before she could draw her weapon. She collapsed to the floor as blood streamed from her forehead.

An alarm blared, ringing through the building like the bugles of Hell. Reed's heart thumped, and each breath was strained beneath the constricting body armor. He knelt and snatched the keycard from the hip of the unconscious agent, then held the gun into his shoulder and orbited the corner toward the hallway. Steel doors guarded the entrance to the elevators and the stairwell. Both were controlled with keycard access.

Reed slid the card at the stairwell and waited for the green light to shine, then jerked the door open and thundered up the stairs. With each footfall, fresh adrenaline surged into his system. Thoughts of Banks and the ukulele on top of the parking garage faded from his mind and were replaced by the overwhelming urge to conquer. Combat was what he knew best. It didn't matter if he was kicking down wooden doors in Iraq or glass office doors in Georgia; the explosive thrill of fear and anticipation felt the same. It was a high like nothing a narcotic could deliver.

Overhead, agents shouted, and the continuous honk of the alarm filled the stairwell. He took the steps two at a time, making it to the landing of the second floor just as the door burst open and a sandy-haired man wearing a suit and wielding a pistol appeared. The agent wrapped his finger around the trigger and squeezed. Reed slid to his knees, raised the KRISS, and fired twice. The bullets smacked home, directly into the agent's exposed chest. He was knocked off his feet and catapulted out the door. The pistol clattered to the floor, and Reed jumped back to his feet, breaking into a run up the next flight of stairs. More agents confronted him halfway to the next landing, both screaming for him to stop.

They opened fire, and one bullet smacked Reed in the middle of the chest, slamming into the body armor at over a thousand feet per second. The next slug grazed his right arm, shredding the thin shirt and drawing blood. Pain erupted from his torso in torrential waves, ripping through his body and almost knocking him off his feet. Reed grunted through gritted teeth, then lunged forward and grabbed the first agent by the forearm. He ducked low and jerked backward. The agent lost his balance and tumbled over Reed's back before crashing down the stairwell.

Reed stumbled backward and dropped the gun. It dangled from the sling as he delivered a lightning punch to the second man's exposed rib cage. The agent collapsed forward, screaming in pain. He fired again as he fell, but the round flew wide and struck the concrete wall in a shower of white powder.

Everything descended into a blur of blood and pain and adrenaline. Reed followed the punch with a palm strike to the agent's ear, driving his head into the block wall, and bone met concrete with a sickening crack. The agent's eyes rolled back, and he slumped to the floor.

Next level. Cover your ass.

Reed jerked his weapon free of the fallen agent's sport jacket and raised it to eye level as he ran around the next landing. His arm throbbed, and blood dripped from his elbow. Each inhale was agony from the massive bruising inflicted by the chest-armor strike. He wouldn't die, but it would hurt like hell for a few days. He felt the smooth contour of the trigger under his finger, and the fear faded from his mind—a receding tide, leaving nothing but blinding determination behind it.

A large number four was painted on the wall in

gleaming white stencil. Sirens and shouts echoed from the other side of the door as Reed fired three rounds into the lock. It blew to pieces in a shower of sparks and shrapnel, and he kicked it open.

The noise on the other side of the door was much louder. Red lights flashed overhead, and complete chaos ruled the room around him. Reed raised the rifle and flipped the selector switch to full auto before unleashing a string of rounds over the tops of a dozen cubicles. Somebody screamed over the familiar popping of a 9mm handgun. Bullets skipped against the wall nearby, and Reed slid to his knees and redirected his line of fire at a short female agent who stood ten yards away between the cubicles. Reed trained the gun on her chest and squeezed the trigger, delivering a 255-grain, lead-nose bullet into the center mass of her Kevlar body armor. She crumpled like a rag doll.

The air hung thick with gun smoke. Blood puddled on the floor around Reed as he opened fire on the walls and the ceiling, shattering lights and alarm sirens. Sparks and drywall debris rained down on the office in a cloud of white before the gun's bolt locked back on empty. Reed pulled himself to his feet and dropped the mag. He slammed a new one in place, smacked his palm against the bolt release, and raised the gun again.

Chaos ruled. Through the smoke and dust, the distinguishable features of the room were seen only through the flashes of handgun fire. The stock of Reed's weapon ground against his cheek as more agents appeared around the corner, fifteen yards away. Both went down before they could even raise their Glocks.

The hellish roar of the submachine gun filled the office space and rattled the windows as brass showered down over the bloody carpet. Reed broke into a run between the offices, leaping across the fallen agents and turning toward the next hallway. A heavy steel door bolted closed with no window or latch blocked the way. Reed dropped the KRISS, allowing it to swing on its harness. Digging into his right cargo pocket, he retrieved a small wad of C-4 and slapped it onto the wall beside the door. He pressed a detonator into the sticky white explosive, flipped the switch, and dove for the floor on the other side of a cubical.

The C-4 discharged with a floor-shaking blast, and an avalanche of concrete, drywall, and rebar cascaded over the carpet around him. Reed felt something slam into his leg, and at first thought it was a piece of debris. Then he heard another gunshot. He groaned and rolled over. Blood coated his leg and mired the carpet, causing him to slip as he struggled to get to his feet. His vision blurred, and the room around him swayed and danced as though an earthquake had erupted under the building. His hands shook, and he spat dirt and saliva onto the carpet.

Reed fought to raise the rifle, but the sling was tangled around his arm and hung on the gun belt. He could see the shooter now, standing next to the elevator and firing from the cover of an upturned desk. Muzzle flash lit up the smoke-filled room in little orange bursts as bullets smacked the wall around him. Reed clawed the Glock out of his drop holster and raised it, firing five times. The fast-shooting .357 caliber slugs sent splinters of fake wood flying as the agent dove for better cover.

The room was dark now and clouded with dust. Reed coughed and holstered the handgun, jerking the KRISS back to his shoulder before turning toward the hole left by the blast of the explosives. It was about two feet across, torn through the block as though a giant had put his fist through the wall. Lights flashed on the other side. Agents shouted, and footsteps pounded the carpeted floor.

Stepping up beside the hole, Reed winced at the pain in his leg. It throbbed and burned. His fingers trembled with the mad rush of adrenaline and the unbridled desire to survive as he jerked a flashbang from his chest rig, pulled the pin with his teeth, and flung it through the hole.

The grenade detonated with an earthshaking blast only a moment later. Reed didn't wait. He held the KRISS close to his chest and dove through the hole.

On the other side of the wall, a large and linear room with stark-white walls and a series of reinforced glass partitions greeted him. The floor was covered in concrete and dirt, and a small table lay on its side. People shouted from somewhere on the other side of the room. The air smelled dirty and burnt, as though he were breathing in ashes. His lungs were clogged with the filth.

Reed rolled into a crouching position and raised the gun. He fired into the glass panels separating him from the far side of the building. They shattered, leaving the wire reinforcements floating in midair behind them.

Glass rained down, and people continued to shout. Gunshots rang out from the far end of the building, and this time they weren't the rapid pops of a handgun. This gunfire was both faster and louder. It was from an assault rifle.

More glass shattered, and pieces of foam exploded from the cubical partitions under the raking fire of the rifle. Reed pulled another flashbang from his chest and flung it as far toward the other end of the building as possible. Before it detonated, he followed it up with the smoke grenade.

The room reverberated with the blast of the first grenade, followed by the slow hiss of the second. The fire alarm overhead began to scream, the sprinkler system kicked in, and cool water showered down. Reed jumped to his feet and ran toward the end of the hallway, where he held the rifle up to his cheek. Agents coughed, and somebody shouted for backup. Reed slid around the corner of one of the glass partitions and saw a tall man leaning over, coughing onto the floor with an assault rifle held loosely in his arms.

Before he could lift the weapon, Reed twisted the butt of the submachine gun in an elegant arc and slammed it into the agent's face. The man went down like a house of cards, crumpling to the floor without a sound.

More gunfire rang through the room. Reed returned fire, though he couldn't see what he was aiming at through the dense smoke. Somebody shouted, and he heard the familiar thud of his bullets striking body armor.

A body hit the floor. Bullets whistled past his ear.

This is going sideways, fast. I've got to move.

The roar of a shotgun shook the walls of the narrow room. Two rounds of the heavy buckshot struck Reed in the stomach of his body armor panel. He choked and stumbled as bile and chunks of steak spewed from his mouth. He squeezed the trigger of the KRISS, the gun jerked, and then the bolt locked back on empty. Extreme pain cascaded through his body, but Reed repeated his reloading routine. Saliva dripped from his lips, and his knees wobbled under him as he staggered forward again.

The smoke began to clear, and Reed saw two men huddled behind a copy machine. A third man lay against the wall in the corner, clutching his chest. A woman was crumpled on the floor next to another reinforced door. This time, though, the door wasn't locked. It hung open a couple of inches, and through the gap, Reed saw the frightened eyes and washed-out face of Mitchell Holiday.

17

Holiday sat in a folding chair with his hands cuffed to the tabletop and his face spotlighted beneath the LED lights. In a millisecond, Reed noted every detail of the predicament, and his stomach fluttered.

Why is Holiday handcuffed?

Gunshots popped from the crowd of disoriented agents. Reed rolled behind a desk and jerked his last flashbang from his chest rig. He hurled it over the desk and covered his head. The room shook, and glass showered the dirty carpet. Reed jumped up, raised the KRISS, and placed a string of shots just over the heads of the stumbling FBI agents. They ducked and screamed, raising their hands over their heads as the guns began to drop.

Reed rushed the disoriented agents and slammed the butt of his gun into the stomach of the nearest one, causing her to double over. He followed the blow with a palm strike to her exposed head, and she collapsed to the floor just as a bullet slammed into his backplate. As if he were hit with a sledgehammer, waves of agony ripped through his torso. He twisted to the left just in time to miss the next bullet.

The shooter stood ten feet away, firing from between the cubical walls. Reed jerked the Glock from his thigh and shot twice. The agent crumpled to the floor with blood spraying from his right arm, and the final agents clawed their way out of the room, coughing and falling over each other.

I've got to extract. Now.

Reed turned toward the metal door and kicked it open.

Holiday stood up, jerking at the cuffs. He stumbled over his own feet and shouted, "Don't shoot!"

Reed jerked the submachine gun back to his shoulder and fired twice. The chain linking the hand-cuffs shattered, and Holiday collapsed against the wall with a panicked shout.

The folds of the senator's collar were soaked with sweat, and Reed dug his fingers into Holiday's neck, hoisting him to his feet before jamming the muzzle of the gun into his ribs. "Do exactly as I say. Don't scream."

The look in his wild eyes told Reed he wouldn't resist. This man was beyond terrified and on the verge of a total psychotic breakdown. Reed shoved him toward the nearest window and looked out over the senator's shoulder. Fifteen feet below them, just across a five-foot alley, was the flat-topped roof of a two-story shopping strip. A ladder hung off the far side of the building, leading down to where Reed parked the SUV.

Boots thundered up the stairwell behind them. Men shouted, and more sirens blared.

I'm so sick of sirens.

Turning back to the window, he fired three rounds into the thick glass and was gratified to see it shatter. A few swift kicks removed the remaining shards, leaving a wide hole into the open air outside.

"Hold your arms to your chest," Reed snapped. "Run and jump."

Holiday shook his head. "No way!"

Reed pulled the trigger of the gun twice, and the laminate flooring erupted in a haze of dust next to Holiday's feet. The senator jumped and held up his hands again.

"Jump. Now!" Reed shouted.

Holiday hesitated, then glanced toward the stairwell and back at Reed holding the gun.

The senator flung himself through the window, and Reed watched him hurtling through the air like a lame duck, arms and legs flailing before he crashed onto the pea gravel of the flat roof. There was a snapping sound on impact, and Holiday screamed and grabbed at his knee.

A flashbang detonated from the other side of the door. Reed's ears rang, and his head was light, as though it were filled with helium. He blinked back the mist of confusion, then launched himself through the window. Clear air and bright sunlight flashed past him as he fell forward, preparing himself for a parachute landing as the roof of the shopping center rocketed toward him. Gravel and dirt crunched under his shoulder, and he rolled once before hauling himself to his feet, just yards from Holiday. His head still swam, and every step was uncertain, as though he were walking on a cloud.

Blood coated the gravel under Reed's boots as he stepped over Holiday and grabbed him by the collar again. "Get up! Move!"

Holiday's eyes were clamped shut, as though he had decided the world couldn't hurt him if he couldn't see it. He cried out in pain at the pressure on his neck but limped to his feet.

Reed shoved him toward the ladder, continuing to shout and prod him with the submachine gun. "Move, Senator!"

Holiday went down the rusty ladder first, fumbling with shaky hands and groaning with each step on his right knee. Reed followed just above him, keeping the gun pointed at his head. The ladder stopped ten feet above the sidewalk, and Reed pressed his boot into Holiday's shoulder, forcing him to drop. Even Reed winced when Holiday landed on both feet and screamed in agony.

His knee must be shattered.

Torrents of pain ran through Reed's body as he fell to the street.

"Let's go!" He hoisted Holiday into a semi-standing

position and dragged him around the corner of the shopping mall to the SUV. Holiday's shoes scraped on the ground, and the blood drained from his face, leaving him ashen white and barely conscious.

Reed jerked the rear door of the Toyota open and hoisted Holiday into the back. He crashed into the cargo space with a pained groan, and Reed shoved Holiday's legs in, then lifted the butt of the gun.

"I'm sorry, Senator."

Another flash of fear crossed across Holiday's face, but he didn't have time to shield himself. The butt of the gun smacked him in the base of the skull, and he fell limp in the cargo space. Reed slammed the door shut and then ran to the driver's seat. His fingers trembled as he fought with the ignition wires. Fire alarms still rang from the building and were now joined by the whine of a fire truck siren. The SUV sputtered to life, and Reed planted his foot into the accelerator. In the rearview mirror, the FBI field office was shrouded by smoke. The slow whoop of a police siren joined the fire truck. Or was it several sirens? They were closing in on his position like hounds racing after a rabbit.

For all of that, no black SUVs swerved to follow him. No helicopters buzzed down on him like vultures, ready to gun him down in a shower of lead. The street ahead lay empty, providing a clear avenue of escape.

Reed winced as a stabbing pain shot through his rib cage. His lips were dry, and he dug a half-empty bottle of water from the door pocket of the SUV and guzzled it down. The fresh taste washed away the dust and bile, dampening his dry throat and promising new life for his battered body.

Blood loss. Bruised ribs, or maybe broken ones. At least one definite bullet strike in his lower leg. Plenty of strained muscles. All things considered, Reed felt lucky. The element of surprise mixed with overwhelming violence and three flashbangs made for a winning cocktail.

He pulled the ski mask off his head and sucked in the fresh air. The SUV didn't smell half bad after the warzone behind him. He turned onto I-85, and the warmth of the sun blazed down on the back of his neck. It was strangely relaxing, in spite of the reminder that darkness was barely ninety minutes away. With a little more luck, it would be time enough.

The buildings around him gradually gave way to rising hills and trees as he passed through Buckhead and turned toward Doraville. Ten minutes later, the green signs on the side of the highway advertised exits for Duluth and Lawrenceville. Reed took the ramp onto Georgia State Highway 316 and continued east. Occasional cars passed him, piloted by tired men in business suits and stressed soccer moms with frazzled hair. Nobody gave a second glance to the stolen Toyota or the killer who sat behind the wheel. As the cityscape gave way to horse fields and peach orchards, the BMWs were replaced by pickup trucks and large SUVs, but the faces remained the same: detached and uninterested.

After another half hour, he turned onto a dirt road and drove a couple more miles. Pine trees and dense, dying undergrowth clogged the fields on either side of him, encroaching on the orange roadbed like the claws of nature, ready to swallow it whole. An armadillo scampered across the road, its tail dragging in the dust and sending orange clouds rising in the face of the Toyota. Birds flitted between the trees, singing songs of impending winter and nesting down for the night. The isolation was perfect, and it brought calm back to Reed's strained mind. He relaxed in his seat and loosened the body armor, which allowed him to take his first real breath in hours. It hurt like hell, but the oxygen brought welcome relief to his frayed nerves.

I'm not dead, neither is Banks, and neither is Holiday. I'm regaining control.

Reed turned the SUV off the road and onto a narrow trail, barely marked by shallow ruts. Branches scraped against the side of the SUV as he lurched over potholes and fallen tree limbs. Around a bend, a locked cattle gate blocked the way.

Reed got out of the Toyota and pulled a key from his pocket. The rusty lock binding the gate to a half-rotten fence post squeaked and stuck, but Reed jerked it open and shoved the gate out of the way. Back in the SUV, he wound his way another half mile into the trees.

The single-wide trailer sat by itself in a clearing barely large enough to hold it. There was no driveway or parking space, no mailbox or front lawn. Faded yellow sheet metal clung to the sides of the trailer, showing traces of rust amid the dents and scratches. Pine needles and small limbs were piled high on the flat roof, and what was left of a narrow front porch leaned to one side, with a chunk of the rail missing. The battered home looked tired and broken as if nobody had laughed or shared a beer with a friend in this place for a long, long time.

Reed got out of the SUV and looked up. The sun descended into the western sky, sending stunning rays of gold, orange, and red streaming through the trees like a continuous burst of fireworks. He opened the rear hatch and pulled Holiday out. The senator was still unconscious, with saliva draining out of his mouth. Reed checked his pulse, then slung the inert lawmaker over his shoulder and dragged him up the front steps and onto the rickety porch. The damp smell of rotting wood and musty insulation filled his nostrils, and he coughed as he shoved another key into the deadbolt. It twisted with a dry squeak, then the door swung open, revealing a pitch-black living room on the other side. Reed drew the flashlight from his belt and flipped it on, then dragged Holiday inside.

The trailer belonged to Oliver's company; one of a network of safe houses and hideouts littered across the country. Both the trailer and the half-acre it sat on were registered in the name of a Georgia LLC, which was owned by a Kansas LLC, which was owned fifty-fifty by two Montana LLCs, and so on—a typical procedure for company property. Reed had never used it before, but he always kept it in the back of his mind in case there came a time when he needed to lay low close to Atlanta.

A time such as this.

The floor shuddered and creaked as though it

might collapse as Reed dropped Holiday onto the torn linoleum. He walked into the kitchen and shuffled through the drawers, dumping plastic forks and rat poop onto the counter, until he found a wooden spoon. He drew the Ka-Bar from his belt and whittled the end of the spoon's handle into a sharp point, about the same diameter as a .30 caliber bullet. Then he returned to the living room and knelt beside Holiday.

Empty darkness filled the senator's eyes. He lay on the floor with his arm twisted under him, his jaw slack. Reed drew a small bottle of ether from his pocket and held it under Holiday's nose, waiting for his breaths to become more consistent. When he was confident the senator was well and truly incapacitated, he stretched the front of Holiday's dress shirt and lifted the sharpened spoon. Two swift stabs to the chest left twin holes just above Holiday's heart, about half an inch deep and three inches apart. Blood pooled out of the holes, soaking the shirt and draining onto the floor.

Reed stood and tossed the spoon into the corner, then drew his phone from his pocket and held the flashlight over the body. The LED glow shone on Holiday's face, washing his skin in a chalky pallor. Reed snapped a few pictures from different angles then reviewed each one. The effect was perfect. Holiday lay on the floor with two bullet-sized wounds streaming blood over his chest.

A thick wad of stuffing from the broken armchair in the corner subdued the bleeding. Reed bound it in place with strips from Holiday's undershirt and propped his body against the wall so the blood would run downward and away from the wounds. Then he selected the unknown number from his recent-callers list and sent a string of photographs followed by one message.

IT'S DONE.

18

Outside of Atlanta, Georgia

The last rays of sunlight faded through the pines. Reed stood amid the trees and lit a cigarette, enjoying the tangy flood of nicotine as it washed through his lungs, bringing fresh waves of relief along with it. The throbbing ache in his body subsided a little, and he exhaled through his nose. So many times, he swore off cigarettes. So many times, he enjoyed a "last smoke ever." The habit started in Iraq, where booze was restricted and tobacco was cheap. That first smoke became a pack a day in less than a month. Careful restraint reduced the addiction to a pack per week, but he couldn't fully surrender the comfort of the smoldering drug. Not yet.

Not until I'm home.

Careful inspection of his body confirmed that he wasn't seriously injured. His chest and back were bruised, and his ears rang. The bullet strike on his leg was a graze, and quick attention with the first aid kit in his cargo pants pocket stopped the bleeding. For now, that would have to suffice.

His cell phone buzzed. UNKNOWN lit up the screen. Reed took another slow pull of smoke, then hit the green button. "It's done. Where's Banks?"

Salvador spoke calmly, disguising a hint of venom beneath his words.

"Impressive work, Montgomery. I'll be honest. I wasn't sure you could pull it off. He certainly looks dead . . ."

Salvador let his voice trail off, leaving the sentence hanging. The suspicion was evident in his tone.

"He's dead. And you will be too if you don't hold up your end. Where's Banks?"

"Hmm . . ."

Reed's heart pounded, and he slammed his clenched fist against the nearest pine tree, but he didn't speak. This was a battle of nerves, and he wouldn't be the one to break.

"In your original contract, you may recall we had a stipulation for the manner of death."

Reed searched his memory, trying to remember the details of that first contract.

"You wanted him dead within seventy-two hours. And he is."

"Right. But we also specified that the death had to be *conspicuous*."

"I just knocked down a freaking FBI stronghold, you cheap shit. How much more conspicuous can you get?"

"Granted. But we're going to need more. Where's the body now?"

"Someplace the FBI isn't."

"I figured as much. We're going to need more concrete assurances of his death. Along with a more public . . . spectacle. Are you following me, Reed?"

"No. I'm not. And I'm done playing games. He's dead. I'm coming for Banks. Where is she?"

Salvador sighed. "Reed . . . you challenge my patience. Hit her."

Reed heard an abrasive popping sound . . . an unearthly scream . . . a muffled crashing . . . another scream.

"Stop." Reed didn't shout. Blood thundered in his ears, and his throat was dry, but he forced himself to focus. There was no card for him to play. He could bluster and threaten all he wanted, but at the end of the day they both knew he was helpless.

The screaming faded, and Salvador returned. "As I was saying. We want a spectacle. I'm feeling generous. It's just now five o'clock, and I'll give you until ten."

"What do you want?"

"I want you to tie a rope around Holiday's ankles and hang his body off the west side of the 191 Peachtree building."

Ice-cold dread washed through Reed's body, landing in his stomach and triggering a wave of nausea. "*What*?"

"You heard me, Reed. I want you to present his body in front of CNN headquarters."

"That building is secured access. I can't get inside.

I'll display the body in Centennial Park. Or on the Capitol steps."

"No. I want it done at 191 Peachtree. And I want it on an upper floor. Shall we say the forty-fifth floor? That seems reasonable."

Reed slammed his closed fist into the hood of the SUV, clenching his jaw to avoid screaming. The frustration and tension in his body overwhelmed him. It rushed through his blood and clouded his mind in a wave of total rage.

"I can't get inside. It can't be done."

Another laugh. It was a dry, humorless sound.

"Reed, you just knocked down an FBI stronghold. An office building should be a walk in the park. You have five hours. Oh, and Reed?"

"What?" Reed spat the word.

"Make it bloody."

19

Special Agent Matthew Rollick sat in his windowless cubical and watched his computer screen in silence as the soundless security camera played footage in black-and-white with poor resolution. Parts of it were obscured by smoke, and some of the camera angles prevented him from viewing the face of the man in the ski mask. He wondered if that was intentional. Did the masked attacker purposefully dodge the cameras, or was it just his own crappy luck?

Rollick clicked the ballpoint pen in his hand and replayed the tape. His T-shirt clung to his skin, and he flipped the desk fan to a higher speed. It didn't help much. The AC unit was out again.

First, he viewed the receptionist. As the glass door of the field office swung open, she had stepped back, assumed a fighting stance, and reached for her gun. There were two flashes from the muzzle of the submachine gun in the attacker's hands, and she went down. Then the stairwell. The cameras provided a limited view of the gunfight between the first and fourth floors. More gunshots. Three agents down.

And then—in what couldn't be described as anything less than a massacre—the entire fourth floor was overtaken and subdued by the one man and his gun.

Rollick punched the blinking call-waiting button on his desk phone. The name flashing on the screen read "Fleet, L."

"Okay. I watched it," Rollick said.

"What do you think?" Agent Lucas Fleet's voice carried an oppressive Boston accent, mixed with the rasp of too many cigarettes.

Rollick leaned back in his chair and hooked his forearm behind his head. "I think, whoever he is, he eats his green vegetables."

"No kidding."

"How many causalities?"

Lucas grunted. "That's the crazy part. None."

"Say what?"

"None. I mean, we've got some pretty banged-up agents. Lots of broken ribs, shattered eardrums, etcetera. A couple gunshot wounds in the shoulders and arms, but no fatalities."

"I don't understand. He shot at least four agents, center mass."

"Yep. But the only bullets that struck a vital area were all stopped by body armor. They shattered some bones and left some bruises, but they didn't penetrate. We're still running tests, but initial impressions are that they were lead-nose bullets."

Rollick scratched his jaw. "That's a miracle."

"Maybe. Or maybe not."

"Come again?"

"Every round was placed squarely in the center of the vests, right where the Kevlar would absorb the bulk of the shock. It's unlikely that any .45-caliber cartridge would penetrate body armor, but it's almost certain that a lead-nose bullet wouldn't. If I'm going to war, and I'm trained well enough to take out a dozen FBI agents, I'm not loading my gun with lead-nose bullets."

"Unless you didn't actually want to kill anyone." Rollick finished the thought.

"Exactly."

"You did say there were some gunshot wounds."

"Yep. A few. All flesh wounds, nothing fatal."

Rollick unwrapped a peppermint candy and popped it between his lips. "What's your theory?"

"I don't have one. That's why I called you. You've been working this Holiday case for three months. I hoped you might have some ideas."

Rollick placed his right hand behind his head and twisted his neck until it popped, providing moderate relief for his sore muscles. His head hurt. He knew there were dark circles under his eyes, and he wasn't really sure what day it was. Friday, maybe? He couldn't remember his last shower, either, but none of this was unusual. He had indeed worked the Holiday case for three months, and holy mackerel, what a nightmare. Endless dead ends, missing emails, corrupted surveillance footage, silent witnesses, and vanishing suspects. It was the most frustrating, exhausting case he had ever worked. Holiday had been a top witness— and possible suspect—for the previous ten weeks, but he was impossibly hard to crack. Rollick's fifteen years as an investigator taught him the unique stench of fear. Holiday was drenched with it.

"I don't know, Lucas. I talked to Holiday for about half an hour before your boys picked him up. He was agitated, but that's typical with him. He's got this goddaughter that he's really close to. Frank Morccelli's girl. He wanted all these guarantees of her isolation from the case and the media. Of course, I couldn't promise that, so he hung up. An hour later, I got word that you had him under protective custody for the death threat."

"Hit order," Lucas corrected him. "And yeah, I'm sorry I didn't advise you beforehand. There wasn't much time. He was a bit contentious, also. We had to restrain him in the safe room."

"It's fine. I can assume that whoever is on the other side of this mess got word Holiday was about to squeal, and they wanted him buried. That would make the fifth witness to vanish or bite the dirt right before they talked."

"You think our gunman is employed by your suspects?"

"I don't have any suspects. Just a series of crimes that feel linked to me, and a gut feeling that there's a bigger picture behind it all. Holiday claims he has insider knowledge about a massive conspiracy, and he also claims to have damning proof. But he won't share it until I meet his demands. This incident adds fuel to the fire, but even so, I'm not sure this gunman works for whoever Holiday wants to rat on."

"Why's that?" Rollick could hear Lucas grinding his thumb against a cigarette lighter.

Geez, the man never quit.

"Because he didn't kill him," Rollick said. "If they wanted him eliminated, it would've been easy to do. I mean, our security obviously isn't an issue. So why kidnap him?"

Lucas breathed out, and Rollick imagined he could smell the sordid odor of cigarette smoke. Seconds turned into minutes, punctuated by occasional puffs from Lucas. He must've been re-watching the security footage for the umpteenth time.

"Maybe they wanted to talk to Holiday first. Make sure he hadn't leaked anything."

"That's possible, but most of my witnesses have a habit of simply winding up dead. Still, he's a state senator. Maybe they're being more surgical this time."

Lucas was quiet a moment longer, and Rollick heard the clicking of a computer mouse.

"What strikes you about him?" Lucas said. "The gunman."

The security footage played on loop now, starting with the carnage in the lobby and moving to the stairwell. Rollick studied the attacker's moves—the way he managed his weapons, his stance, dress, and tactics. They weren't the stuff of an action movie, but they were brutally effective.

"Military," he said.

"Yep. And look at his stance. Adjusted Weaver-style,

maintaining his hold on the grip of the gun when he changes mags, leaning low against the walls . . ."

"He's one of ours," Rollick finished.

"Looks that way. Not your average GI, though."

"So, we have another rogue spec ops commando on our hands."

Lucas grunted. "Yep. Okay, Roll. I'll keep you posted if we make any progress. Get some shut-eye. You sound like death."

The line went dead, and Rollick leaned back and rubbed his eyes. Coming from Lucas, the prognosis was as good as a terminal illness.

20

D arkness blanketed the forest, saturating the clearing and leaving Reed alone in the cold. The air was thin but smelled heavily of pine needles. As the last of the sun vanished over the horizon, the tension in his chest increased, and cold sweats ran down his back. The Kevlar suffocated him, and he jerked it off and hurled it to the ground with a scream.

"*Dammit!*" Reed drove his fist into the hood of the SUV again, leaving a large dent. He gasped for air and leaned over the Toyota, resting his forehead against the cool metal. A light breeze whispered through the forest, and it felt good to breathe it in.

Banks was alone. A captive of the freak from South America. A madman with an obsessive desire to destroy her godfather. *Why?* The thought wouldn't leave his mind. Why the *hell* did they want him so publicly executed? Of all the twisted, depraved crap they could come up with—hanging his body off the side of a skyscraper? It was beyond bizarre and worse than twisted. It was sickening.

Pine needles and dry sticks crunched under his feet as Reed straightened. He paced in front of the trailer as his eyes adjusted to the darkness. His mind raced as he considered his options—not that he had many. He couldn't kill Holiday, of course. And he couldn't throw him off the 191 building.

Again, the keystone of the problem was the request itself—their obsession with a conspicuous death didn't add up. Holiday's violent kidnapping and disappearance were conspicuous enough—maybe the most conspicuous thing Reed had ever done. By sunrise, every news outlet in the country would carry the story. The nation would dissolve into a state of shock as pundits and talk show hosts fanned the flames of public uncertainty into a roaring blaze of fear. The president would make a thoughts-and-prayers speech, then call the director of the FBI and demand immediate answers.

So why inflame things any further? Amplifying the horror of the murder now only stacked the deck against these people in every possible way. A gruesome and public display of the body would all but ensure that the killer was run down and . . .

Reed stopped pacing, and a tingling sensation rippled up his arms. There it was. It was so painfully obvious. They *wanted* the killer to be caught. And that killer was him. The whole thing was an elaborate setup. Salvador wanted him to be apprehended at the FBI building. He probably laid a trap at the Ikea, also. When Reed evaded capture both times, they had no choice but to up the ante once more. Naming the place and time of Holiday's post-mortem display was a perfect way to ensure success. Reed would be cornered on the 45th floor of a secured-access building with no route of escape. One call to the Atlanta PD, and the music would stop. Reed would be caught in the act, as guilty as sin.

Like cops closing in on an escaped prisoner, the darkness enveloped his mind, making him feel suddenly smothered. Reed fell to the ground and slumped against a tree, burying his face in his hands. Images of Banks's bright smile flooded his mind, pushing past his most desperate attempts to block them out. He imagined the face of her captor, his teeth narrowing into fangs as he pressed a knife into her stomach. Her smile turned to screams as she fought, begged, screamed.

Reed was cornered, and it was his own fault. Every step over the last twenty-four hours had led him deeper into the muck. It was a trap from the start, and his moronic refusal to look after his own interests had ensured that he fell head over heels into the pit.

He jumped to his feet and turned back to the trailer, flipping the flashlight on. The dark living room still smelled musty and stale, with a hint of blood in the air. Reed shuffled through the kitchen drawers again until he located a bottle of water and half a roll of duct tape. Both were old and dirty, but serviceable.

Strips of tape secured Holiday's hands to his thighs,

and a third locked his ankles together. Reed slipped the ski mask back on, then opened the water bottle and dumped it over his prisoner's face while smacking him on the cheeks. The senator coughed and blinked bloodshot eyes full of fear when he recognized the black ski mask, and he mumbled a panicked plea before recoiling from the water. Reed shoved the bottle into Holiday's mouth.

"Drink," he snapped.

Holiday didn't object. He gulped the water, spluttering as it streamed down his chin. Reed let him consume all but the last swallow, then finished the rest himself.

"Where am I?"

It was a predictable question.

"West Virginia," Reed said without hesitation. He needed Holiday to talk, and he guessed the senator would respond best to open dialogue.

"Why?"

Reed squatted in front of him. The senator still appeared confused, as though he wasn't aware that he had been kidnapped. But the rasping breaths and rigid posture betrayed his terror.

"I brought you here. Now you're going to answer some questions. Do you understand?"

Holiday grunted. His eyes began to clear, but he still wouldn't meet Reed's gaze.

"A hit was placed on your life," Reed said. "Do you understand what that means?"

Something flashed across Holiday's face. Uncertainty? A distant connection, perhaps? He glared at Reed.

"Who are you?"

"I'm the man hired to kill you."

Holiday leaned back and tried to jerk his hands free. It was a futile effort, and Reed pinned him against the wall with one hand.

"Why do they want you dead, Senator?"

Holiday shook his head. "I don't know. You don't want to do this!"

"You're right. I don't. So, answer my question. Who wants you dead?"

Holiday looked away and coughed over the floor. "Look, this isn't worth it. Just walk away while you can."

"Walk away from what?"

"I'm not saying a damn thi—"

Reed cocked his right arm and dealt Holiday a quick punch to the jaw. The cracking sound of bone on bone popped through the small room. Holiday's head smacked into the fake wood paneling of the walls, and blood streamed from his lip as he cried out in pain.

"Don't test me, Senator. Who ordered the hit?"

Holiday spat again, spraying blood and saliva over the dingy linoleum. "How would I know? You think I have any idea how deep this goes?"

"How deep *what* goes?"

Tears mixed with blood as they dripped off Holiday's chin and splashed on his pants. He shook his head again, looked up, and started to answer, but his eyebrows furrowed, and the sobbing faded. He stared at Reed as though he were seeing him for the first time.

"Did you kill Frank?"

The question took Reed off guard. "Who?"

"You son of a bitch. You killed him, didn't you?"

Holiday spat blood in Reed's face. He began to kick out with both legs, thrashing around on the floor of the trailer. His bound feet struck Reed in the knee, and Reed stumbled back with a grunt of pain. The next kick landed in Reed's lower back, sending waves of pain ripping up his spine. Reed threw himself on top of Holiday and sent another powerful punch into the senator's throat. Holiday choked and coughed up blood, gasping for breath. Reed hit him again in the face, leaving a swollen red welt on his right cheekbone.

"Who are they? Who wants you dead?" Reed shouted.

It was pointless. Holiday slumped forward, his face as white as a corpse. Reed grabbed his wrist and felt a pulse, but the senator was out cold.

Perfect.

Reed let him fall to the floor with a meaty thud, then stood up and jerked the ski mask off. He paced the dingy carpet, his heart thumping. He pulled his phone out and redialed Oliver. This time it went directly to voicemail.

There was no hiding from the truth he'd suspected all day. This whole miserable mess was an elaborate puppet show designed to end the moment Reed pressed the trigger outside of Holiday's condo. Whoever ordered this hit—whoever was behind the fear in Holiday's eyes—that person wanted Reed to take the fall for it. They wanted a clean, clear-cut killing. An execution.

Reed leaned against the counter and tried to control his breathing, forcing himself to take slower, calmer breaths. His heart rate slowed, and his mind began to clear. It wasn't all at once, but the thoughts that screamed inside his head became more orderly. More discernible.

I'm alone. Mitchell Holiday is a dead man walking. After him, they'll kill Banks. Then they'll do their best to kill me. The only way out is to run. Cut bait. Leave Holiday and Banks to their fate and get the hell out of Dodge.

The fire in his blood burned through every part of his body. A numbness overcame his urge to flee, followed by a flicker of hatred. The visceral reaction grew into an inferno of outrage—a blinding desire to destroy. He heard her laugh, and he felt a warm rush at the sound of her beautiful voice. It was a feeling he'd long forgotten in the cold, dark world he lived in. It was a feeling he didn't know existed anymore—a beauty he wasn't sure was real. But he felt it, standing there on the top of that parking garage staring out at the city. It *was* real.

He wasn't walking away from this. He wasn't walking away from anything. He'd burn the whole damn city down if that's what it took. He would kick down every door until he ratted Salvador out of his hole and tore out his throat. He was going to find Banks.

Reed set Holiday in the armchair and stretched a

strip of duct tape over his mouth. He locked the trailer and started toward the SUV.

There would be no going back. No chance to disengage from the carnage he was about to unleash. Now that Salvador dragged Banks into this mess, war was the only option.

21

North Georgia

The cabin was a shadow in the darkness. Reed parked the stolen SUV in the driveway, then pounded up the steps and shoved the door open. Baxter snored on the rug in the living room. He jumped to his feet when Reed burst in, and erupted in angry barks, running to the window and snarling at whatever invisible threat had awakened the monster inside his human friend.

Reed jerked the drawers of his desk open and dumped a pile of books and papers on the kitchen table. He pulled a map of Atlanta from the stack and unfolded it, tracing his finger through the streets of downtown until he stopped at the intersection of Andrew Young International Blvd and Peachtree Street. He stared at the block, his mind racing like a freight train careening off its tracks.

191 Peachtree. Right in the heart of the city.

His heart thumped, and he reached for the bottle of Jack sitting on the desk. After a deep swig, he looked back at the map.

There has to be a way to draw them out. Find a way to corner them.

If he attempted to breach the fifty-story skyscraper at that intersection, he would be in handcuffs with his face in the concrete as soon as he exposed the body. Maybe Salvador even had a few Atlanta cops on the payroll. Perhaps they were standing by, even now, waiting to catch a killer attempting to hang a body off the side of an Atlanta landmark.

Reed checked his watch. Six fifteen. This wouldn't be his first operation executed under the torment of a ticking clock, but this one felt different. The strain on his nerves wore at the corners of his focus, infringing on his ability to think outside the box.

They need a spectacle. They need me cornered. So, I have to corner them.

Reed ran a hand through his hair.

What if I do it? What if I hang Holiday off the tower? If he were unconscious, maybe . . .

No, that was moronic. Salvador wanted Reed caught, and executing the ridiculous assignment as instructed wouldn't result in Banks's release. They would kill her. The only way for this to end would be for Reed to turn the ambush into a counter-ambush somehow. Find a way to catch the tiger by the tail and run him back to his cave.

Reed took another sip of whiskey. What if he traced the call and found out where it was made? No, anybody smart enough to block the caller ID would be smart enough to avoid being traced. He had to lure the tiger out. Catch him in the open.

That's it. It's so simple.

He didn't have to lure the tiger out. The tiger would already be out, on the prowl, waiting and watching to make sure Reed was caught. Reed had evaded capture twice, and Salvador couldn't afford to fail again. He would have men planted downtown— not in the tower, but close by within easy viewing distance.

I'll draw them out. If they think I'm escaping, they'll have no choice but to expose themselves. I'll need to see them before they see me. Someplace close. Someplace tall.

Back to the map. The surrounding blocks were marked with tiny icons, indicating the towers that built the Atlanta skyline. He traced the streets around 191 Peachtree, moving out in every direction. Then his finger stopped at the intersection of Peachtree and Luckie Street.

Perfect.

The pine planks of the cabin floor creaked under his boots as he ran through the kitchen and into the pantry, back through the fake wall, and down the narrow steps into the basement. The single lightbulb still glowed overhead, illuminating the dust that hung in the air. He snatched an empty backpack off the wall and began sweeping gear off the shelves and into the bag. A chest harness with a rappel slide, five hundred feet of static climbing rope, a case holding four encrypted radio headsets, a lock pick kit, a bottle of water, and three magazines loaded with twenty rounds each of .308.

The last item of his gear lay in a case on the table: the sniper rifle. It was heavy under his tired and battered grip, but the weight comforted him. It was his weapon of choice—a precise instrument of judgment.

After closing the entrance to the basement, Reed whistled for Baxter. The bulldog bounded off the couch and trotted into the kitchen. His little eyes blazed with curiosity, and maybe just a hint of fighting fury, almost as if the dog were saying, *Come on, we can take 'em!*

Drool dripped from Baxter's bottom lip, and he cocked his head in confusion. Reed knelt beside him and scratched behind his ears, then rubbed him between his shoulder blades, right where he liked it. Baxter groaned and dropped his butt on the floor.

"Yeah. Guess you know it's going down. In case I don't come back . . . Well, you go get that Frenchie, friend."

Reed patted him on the head, then walked out the front door. The last thing he needed was a little ground support, and he had a pretty good idea of where to find it.

Reed loaded the gear into the SUV and drove back into the city. It took him over an hour to fight his way through traffic and back to where he left the Camaro. After parking the SUV, he retrieved a roll of hundred-dollar bills from the Camaro's glove box and laid them in the seat of the Toyota before pressing a sticky note on top of the money. He retrieved a pen from the console and scrawled a brief note on the yellow paper.

Sorry for everything.

The adrenaline from the maddened afternoon began to wear off, and the extreme pain from his injuries started to rip into his body again. His stomach and chest ached like hell from the bullet strikes on his body armor, and each breath sent a streaking pain shooting down his right side—probably from bruised ribs. The pain would be a lot worse in the morning, and his whole body would be stiff, assuming he lived that long.

Reed shifted into gear and roared back onto the freeway. The Camaro shook, and the exhaust growled like all the demons of Hell reciting a war chant. He loved that sound. It helped him focus on something other than the pain in his body and the strain on his mind. He loved that car.

I hope it's in one piece when this is over.

The familiar hallmarks of Buckhead faded into those of Midtown. Reed exited the freeway and turned the car past the Ikea and toward an older part of town. As he passed a gas station, he stepped on the brake and lowered the windows, surveying the streets and small parks. It took him ten minutes to find a homeless man lying on a park bench; a worn blanket was stretched over his thin body. Reed stopped the Camaro at the edge of the park and climbed out, then pulled the Panthers jacket over his shoulder holster and jogged to the bench.

"Excuse me."

The man sat up and waved a dirty fist at Reed. "Leave me alone! Can't a man sleep in a free country?"

Reed held up one hand. "Chill. I'm just looking for Vince. Do you know him?"

With narrowed eyes, the man tilted his head to one side. "Who's asking?"

Reed drew a couple twenties from his pocket and held them out. "Here. Take this. Where is he?"

The homeless man curled his lip. "You think I'd rat on a brother for forty bucks? Go to hell!"

He stood up and shuffled toward the park.

Reed cursed and started to follow, but a crackling voice rang out from behind him.

"Well, well. If it ain't mister big shot, harassing an honest American down on his luck. You're way out of regs, Marine!"

A short, stocky man with his arms crossed stood twenty feet back. He wore a tattered Falcons hoodie, but his hair was neatly cut, and his face cleanly shaved. He didn't look older than thirty-five, but he had dark eyes and a brutal scar that ran down his left cheek.

Reed took a cautious step forward. "Vince? That you?"

The stocky Marine laughed. "You said to get a haircut."

Reed sighed in relief. "I've been looking for you, Sergeant."

"Well, you found me. What do you want?" Vince was abrupt, but there was no aggression in his voice. Reed offered his hand, but Vince kept his arms crossed.

Reed cleared his throat. "I'll get straight to the point. I'm mixed up in some shit. It's not legal. Somebody I care about is in trouble, and I need your help."

Vince continued to stare, his face blank and emotionless. Reed saw the spiderweb of scars tracing his neck and scalp. A burn mark twisted the flesh beneath his right ear, and discoloration marred his shaved cheeks.

Leftovers from the IED?

Vince grunted. "Who's asking?"

"A fellow Marine," Reed said.

The answer seemed to satisfy Vince. He unfolded his arms and shoved his hands into the pockets of the jacket. "What do you need?"

"I need a diversion. If you have some friends, I could use their help, also. I'll make it worth your while."

Vince let out a low whistle, and Reed looked up to see a small group of men, all dressed in shabby, torn clothes, materialize out of the darkness around him. Their faces were cold and hard, one man was missing an arm, and another wore an eyepatch. They were all filthy, but they all sported impeccable haircuts.

Vince waved his arm as though he were presenting Olympic medalists. "Meet the rifle squad, Jarhead. Somebody need their ass kicked?"

Reed indulged a small smile. "I'll take care of the ass-kicking. I just need help with the smoke and mirrors. I have to warn you; somebody could spend the night downtown for this."

A ripple of condescending laughter passed through the small crowd.

"You mean a warm bed and a hot meal?" somebody said.

"Fair enough. I'm just saying, the police are certain to turn up."

Another ripple of laughter. Reed deemed it to be a good sign and jerked his head toward Vince. The sergeant stepped a few feet away from his men, and Reed lowered his voice.

"I have to make sure you understand. There could be use of deadly force."

Vince motioned to the men, now standing in a circle, their hands in their pockets while they talked quietly. "You see that kid over there?"

A scrawny young man with a neck tattoo stood beneath a tree, huddled over in a threadbare sweatshirt. He laughed at a joke, but the mirth didn't make it to his empty eyes.

"That's Private Becker. He's from Milwaukee. Served in Iraq and got shook up pretty bad. Has all kinds of mental crap going on."

Vince reached into his pocket and drew out a cigarette. He lit it with a brand-new Zippo lighter and took a long pull. After blowing smoke through his nose, he continued.

"Two nights ago, this gangbanger from across town jumped Becker. Tried to take his blanket. Cracked a rib."

Vince met Reed's gaze and spoke without a hint of

hesitation. "We crushed his skull and slung his body in a dumpster."

The sergeant's battle-weary face gleamed in the soft glow of the streetlamps. Reed wasn't sure what he expected when he first met Vince, but this wasn't it. This was cold. Brutal.

Vince took another long pull of the cigarette, then sighed. "America has left us with nothing except each other, Corporal. But what we have, we look after. So cut the crap and tell me what you need."

Reed dug the car keys out of his pocket. "Well, Sergeant. Can you drive a stick?"

22

Atlanta, Georgia

As Atlanta's business district closed shop and commuted home, the nightlife of the old city began to stir. The highways, loaded to capacity with overnight shipping traffic, wound their way through Atlanta like giant snakes, one red and one white. Lights flashed from nightclubs. The spire of the Bank of America Plaza and the crowns adorning the top of 191 Peachtree glowed with amber fire, lighting up the night sky with a blazing reminder that the Empire City of the South was as vibrant and alive as ever.

It was the *alive* part that bothered Reed the most. There would never be an ideal time to execute a plan this bold in the heart of downtown. But at nine p.m., with cops patrolling the downtown streets, couples walking hand-in-hand between ice cream shops, and city buses rolling in and out of their downtown garages, the deck felt stacked against him. Reed's only advantage was the shield of nightfall, but even the darkness was beaten into submission by the blazing streetlamps and flashing headlights.

Reed stood at the edge of the park, huddled close to the shadows, as he stared up at the impending mass of 191 Peachtree, rising from the concrete jungle five hundred yards away. The granite-faced tower stood 771 feet tall, dominating the skyline with imperial majesty. The crowns sitting on top of the building looked like haunting beacons against the grey sky, shining in golden light from the powerful lamps housed within. Everything about the structure boasted power and stability.

Empire.

Reed ducked his head and adjusted the backpack on his shoulder. He still wore the Carolina Panthers jacket and carried a duffle bag in his left hand. It was less conspicuous than the rifle case, but it accomplished the same task. The familiar rush of adrenaline flooded his system as he stepped across Centennial Olympic Park Drive and started down Luckie Street. It was a feeling he'd felt twenty-nine times before, but this time it was different. It wasn't just the weight of impending death tugging at the edge of his focus; the stakes were bigger this time—as was the stage.

A bicycle cop whirred down the sidewalk, and Reed nodded a brief greeting before hurrying past. Dark solar panels adorned the block to his left, lined in ghostly rows under the dark sky. One block farther on, the Holiday Inn Express rose from the sidewalk, its windows gleaming with yellow light as cars passed quietly in front of it along Cone Street. A homeless man stood on the corner, his gaunt cheeks caving in under sharp cheekbones. Reed handed him a ten-dollar bill before he could ask, then he accelerated his pace.

Two more blocks passed under Reed's combat boots before he stopped at the corner of Forsyth and Luckie Streets and tilted his head back.

The Equitable Building dominated the block with 453 feet of tower. Everything about it was dark. Ebony sheathing framed heavily tinted windows. Black doors guarded the main entrance like gates to Hell. Only the tall letters, glowing in soft white light and gracing the top of the tower, broke the pattern: EQUITABLE.

The building looked like the corporate headquarters of a billionaire mob boss—strong, silent, and brooding.

Reed shifted the backpack on his shoulder.

This is it. You can't lose this time.

The thin wire headset was flimsy over Reed's ear, and he twisted the mic close to his mouth, breathing into it until the radio activated. "Vince, you with me?"

"Who's Vince? This is Falcon One, your driver."

"Right. Of course. And my tower team?"

"Call them Falcon Two. Falcon Three has the van. What about you?"

"Prosecutor," Reed said. "My call sign is Prosecutor."

"Roger that, Prosecutor. We're standing by."

The earpiece clicked as Reed muted it. He hurried around the corner and onto the tower's service alley. Shadows danced under the streetlamps as a decorative tree swayed in the night breeze. Machinery hummed from the loading dock, and a black cat scampered across the alley. But there were no people. No security. Reed moved deeper into the shadows and climbed onto the loading dock. His torso erupted in waves of pain as he pulled himself back to his feet. The injuries burned beneath his skin, sending bursts of agony into his skull. The dock wavered under his feet, and Reed leaned against the wall to steady himself. He'd suffered bruises and broken ribs before. There was little to do besides suck it up and press on.

Even though the breeze dropped into the low fifties, Reed was clammy with perspiration as he approached the service door and tried the latch. It was locked, and a cheap, plastic card key reader with a single flashing light was mounted next to the door. Reed flipped his pocket knife out and began to pry the cover off.

"So, Prosecutor." Vince's voice crackled over the headset. "What happened in Iraq?"

Reed paused over the card reader. "Iraq?"

"You said you left the Marines in handcuffs. Sounds like a hell of a story."

Reed hesitated. "Your point?"

"We've got time to kill. What happened?"

The plastic cover snapped off, exposing a small circuit board and several multi-colored wires. Reed stuck his flashlight between his teeth, and with the tip of his knife, he began removing the tiny silver screws that held the circuit board in place.

Reed spoke around the flashlight. "Let's just say . . . the right thing and the legal thing aren't always the same thing."

Vince grunted. "So, you did the right thing, and you went to prison for it."

"Yeah." Reed's focus blurred for a moment. He paused over the card reader as momentary flashes of that dark night in Baghdad reentered his mind. They were as fresh as the moment they transpired. The gunshots. The bodies on the ground. The resulting whirlwind of a court-martial, a prison sentence, the hopelessness of death row.

And then, Oliver. Reed's one chance at freedom.

"Thirty kills in exchange for your freedom."

"Wanna tell me what went down?" Vince asked, jarring Reed out of his thoughts.

Reed blinked his way back into focus and cleared his throat. "Not really."

Vince grunted again. "I get it. Backstory then. Where you from?"

"You first."

"Montana! Big Sky Country. A ranch with a few thousand head of cattle. Grew up wrangling beef and raising hell."

Reed's thoughts cleared as the circuit board fell off, further exposing the wires. Reed slipped the blade under an orange wire and pressed his thumb over the rubber jacketing, applying just enough pressure to expose the copper wire beneath. Two more precise twists of the knife revealed the yellow and black wires. He severed the red wire next and pressed the other three together across their sides. The light flashed green, and the latch clicked.

"You eat a lot of steak in Montana?" Reed said.

"Best damn steak you ever stuck a fork in. I'm a ribeye man myself, but I don't mind a filet now and again."

Reed opened the door and hurried inside, holding the light at shoulder level. A hallway opened up in front of him. It was dark, with thick wooden doors lining either side. Storage closets, maybe. The floor was slick with wax, and his rubber boots squeaked with each footstep.

"Amen to that. Slap it on a plate with a baked potato and salad. Beer or sweet iced tea."

"Iced tea?" Vince laughed. "That's a Southern tradition. You from 'round here?"

Two turns in the hallway brought Reed to an intersection with elevators and a service door. The elevators were locked by card key, as was the stairwell. He could breach them again, but unlike the dock door, these access points probably recorded entry, and there would be surveillance inside the elevators and stairwells. Reed approached the service door instead.

"I went to high school in LA, but before that, we lived in Birmingham. My dad was from a little town called Sylacauga. I wouldn't say I'm Southern."

"You said *was*. Did your old man pass?"

Reed paused at the service door, his hand hanging over the handle. For a moment, he didn't answer, then he reached into his cargo pocket and pulled out a lock pick.

"Something like that. My mom moved us to California. But you know . . . sweet tea follows you."

Vince grunted again. Maybe he knew when to stop pressing. The lock pick slipped into the keyhole, and Reed manipulated the tiny tool with practiced ease. His ribs throbbed with each slow breath, and sweat dripped off his nose and onto his boot. One twist, then a flick of his wrist, and the lock clicked.

"You got a lady, Falcon?" Reed asked.

"You take me for a motard, Prosecutor? I got a whole busload of ladies!"

A flood of musty air rushed from the service room as Reed stepped in. A quick scan with the flashlight revealed a large storage area with mop buckets, tool boxes, and cardboard boxes littering the floor. On the far end of the room a small door about three feet square was framed in the middle of the wall, with a row of buttons lining the wall beside it.

"No, I'm talking about *the* lady. You know. The face you saw when that IED went off."

Vince sighed. It was a quiet sound. Softer than his usual rumbling growl. "Danielle Taylor . . . the most gorgeous woman in Montana."

The twin doors of the service elevator squeaked and groaned. Reed smacked the button to the top floor, then tossed the duffle bag inside the car before bending over and cramming himself in alongside it. A shiver of misery ripped through his body with the motion. It was all he could do not to scream. Each shallow breath further inflamed his swollen and torn muscles. Every tiny movement was a bolt of lightning flashing through his torso, ripping and burning as it went.

"Brunette?" Reed hissed the word through gritted teeth. The elevator groaned then started upward with a screech of metal on metal.

"She was. Chemo took that. But damn, son, it couldn't take her smile. That's the smile I saw when the IED went off."

Somewhere far overhead, the whine of the winch echoed down the elevator shaft. The cramped interior of the car smelled of oil and cleaning supplies, but the metal was refreshingly cool against his skin. *There's always a silver lining.*

"Did she make it?"

"Oh yes." Vince's words were still soft. "For three years. Breast. Lung. Spine. It finally went to her brain. That's what took her. But she gave it a hell of a fight. Not many a jarhead could've held on like my Danielle."

The radio fell silent, and Reed felt the stillness between them hanging over the invisible distance. It was the kind of stillness that falls between two old men sitting over a beer, too rich to be broken.

"You should be proud, Falcon."

"Damn right, Prosecutor. Heaven is proud to have her."

The elevator screeched to a halt. Numbness overwhelmed the sharper edges of the pain now, providing welcome relief but reducing his ability to make precise motor movements. He would need that precision before this night was over. The green LED letters of his watch read 9:39. Only twenty-one minutes until the deadline. His heart thumped, and he adjusted the pistol on his belt, then he pried the doors open. A cool breeze washed over his face as he piled out of the elevator, dragging the bag behind him. Hard concrete, mixed with the grimy crunch of loose dirt, clicked against his combat boots. Reed flipped the flashlight on and scanned the space around him, taking a moment to catch his breath.

The floor was mostly open, with half-built partitions rising at odd intervals between wooden columns. Cans of paint were stacked next to the wall, and piles of rolled carpet lay in what looked like a future hallway. Bare wires hung from the skeleton of a suspended ceiling. The breeze blew in from somewhere overhead, and the air was fresh—cleaner than the gasoline smell of the city streets far below.

"What about you, Prosecutor? Whose face will you see right before this shit plan of yours explodes?"

Reed slipped between the piles of construction materials, testing the floor with his toes before placing his weight on it. A few yards ahead, the primary elevator shaft shot upward through the floor and disappeared into the ceiling. Unfinished drywall clung to the side of the shaft with gaping cracks and water damage decorating the bland white. A single door stood in the backside of the shaft. It was metal and painted brown, with clean white letters stenciled over the middle of it.

ROOF ACCESS.

"I'm alone," Reed said. "It's just me."

"Aw, come on, Prosecutor. There must have been somebody."

Reed hesitated, then sighed. "There was, once. It didn't last long."

"A fellow Marine?"

Reed chuckled. "A car thief. Her name was Kelly."

"Ah. So, this would have been after your little visit to the lockup."

"Yeah, bad company, and all that. Like I said, it didn't last."

Reed stepped up to the door and reached into his pocket for the lockpick.

"What about the other girl?" Vince asked.

"What girl?"

A short, condescending laugh filled the mic. "The girl we're pulling this moronic scheme for. The one you're obsessing over right now."

Reed hid a smirk as he pressed the lockpick into the keyhole and began to manipulate the tool. "I don't know what you're talking about, Falcon."

"Don't bullshit me, kid. There's only one kind of thing that motivates a man to act the fool. It's love. Love of country, love of money, love of something. The only thing I see you loving is another human."

Reed stared at the door, manipulating the lockpick without looking at it. Seconds passed, then he sighed.

"All right. You got me."

"Brunette?" Vince asked.

"Blonde."

"Girlfriend?"

"No. More like . . . somebody I let down. Somebody I should have protected."

"Hmm . . ." Vince's thought trailed off.

Reed guessed that the sergeant wanted to ask more but now wasn't the time or place.

The lock clicked. Reed pulled the door open and hauled himself up the stairs on the other side. Twelve steps, then he reached another metal door. This one was locked from the inside, and a quick flip of his thumb defeated the bolt. As the hinges squeaked, a blast of wind tore through the small gap, flooding his lungs with life. Another fifteen steps lay on the other side of the door, and then the rooftop. Reed sucked in a long pull of fresh air as he pressed through the doorway and stepped onto the tower's roof.

Atlanta lay at his feet, stretching out for miles on every side. As far as he could see, the lights of every suburb, shopping mall, and streetlamp glowed in the darkness as a star-filled cityscape of towers and hotels, office suites and bus stations. The wind carried the distant bustle of six million residents, their barking dogs, and honking cars. A child laughed from somewhere far away, and a door slammed. Reed imagined he could hear music—maybe the thump of a disco. He could hear the hum of a city bus. A city alive with passion and secrets.

And there, towering in the middle of it all, as a proud monument of Southern tradition, was the 191 Peachtree building. Only a few hundred yards away, its flame-finished granite face gleamed in the light of the other skyscrapers. The shadow of each passing cloud flitted across the tinted windows, gracing the majestic structure with a light show of mottled yellow streetlight and white moonlight.

Reed thought it was nothing short of magnificent.

His head swam, and his legs were wobbly as he approached the edge. If you wanted to make a statement the world would never forget, dropping a body off the side of 191 Peachtree was a good place to start.

He stopped, taking a moment to clear his mind before looking down, 453 feet below him, to the cold outline of Forsyth Street. The pavement wavered, making him feel suddenly dizzy. He stepped away from the edge and closed his eyes, releasing the tension in his muscles and calming his pulse.

Dammit. Why couldn't this have been a ground job?

Reed could take the darkness, the blood, the murky water and suffocating heat. Snakes, spiders, and snapping dogs didn't even bother him, but heights . . . heights he could do without.

The duffle bag thudded against the concrete rooftop. Reed pried out the rifle, snapped it together, and then flipped the lens caps off the scope and locked the bipod into place. His hands trembled with anticipation as he settled down behind the weapon and lifted the butt to his shoulder. It felt good to rest his cheek against the stock, and the cool touch of polymer against his skin was more familiar and comforting than a soft pillow. He felt powerful and in control again.

"Prosecutor to all channels, I have obtained overwatch. Operation is a go."

Vince's voice sounded strong and commanding.

"Very good. Falcon Two, this is Falcon One. Confirm, operation is a go. You may breach the granite dildo."

Reed blinked. "Granite dildo? That's what we're calling it?"

A crackling laugh rippled over the headset. "Welcome back to the Corps, Prosecutor!"

23

The wind bit straight through his Panthers jacket, and Reed avoided looking at the clouds, which would only reinforce the illusion that he was about to crash to the street below in a gruesome puddle of blood and gore. Instead, he focused on his position, nestling himself five feet from the edge of the roof. He lay on his stomach with his legs splayed behind him for extra stability. The cold concrete pressed into his rib cage, sending new waves of pain shooting down his spine. Normally, he would have packed a pad of some kind for overwatch duty, but there hadn't been room for it.

Reed flipped the scope's illumination feature on, then swept the red crosshairs across rooftops until they came to rest on the west face of 191 Peachtree.

Drawing in a long breath, he focused on relaxing each muscle group. First his toes, then the soles of his feet. He breathed through his mouth, relishing the relief of each muscle as it loosened. It brought moderate relaxation to his aching body, promising the possibility that he might not die from busted ribs after all. Each breath became deeper and slower than the last, and his heart rate slowed along with them. His entire body rested in a state of calm. Not comfort, by any stretch. But control.

"Falcon Two, this is Prosecutor. Sitrep, over."

"'Sup, Prosecutor." The man on the other end of the radio didn't suppress his heavy Arkansas accent. Vince introduced him as "Snort," a former assistant squad leader during the Vietnam war. Snort was now pushing seventy, but he moved like a man twenty years younger.

"We have gained entry and are preparing to stroke this shaft."

Reed blinked. "Come again?"

Vince laughed, breaking onto the radio without offering a call sign. "They're gonna ride the elevator."

The radio fell silent, and Reed nestled his cheek against the stock again. He looked down at his watch. The green numerals glowed at 9:52. He wanted to urge Snort to hurry the hell up, but he didn't want to deal with the storm of innuendos that would unleash.

Seconds ticked by. Reed swung the crosshairs down the building and toward the east, surveying the streets. A motorcycle passed by on Ellis Street, and a couple of cars cruised in front of 191's primary entrance on Peachtree Street. The rest of the avenues were quiet. A final stillness was closing over the city, bringing with it a welcome release of tension over Reed's nerves.

I know you're out there. I know you're watching. I'm gonna run your rat ass to ground.

"This is Falcon Two. We have reached the forty-fifth floor. All silent so far. Setting up now."

Reed continued his surveillance of the streets around the tower. He paused over every rooftop, every window, and every parking garage—any place that provided the slightest vantage point over the west face of the tower. He saw no one. No dark cars, no men with binoculars, and no snipers hiding in the shadows.

One more pass, and then Reed swung the optic back to the tower and ran the crosshairs down the building. He paused at the entrance. A black Chevy Impala pulled up to the front door of the office building, while across the street, two patrol cars sat at the intersection of Ellis and Peachtree.

"This is Prosecutor. I have three police vehicles in position at the main entrance . . . possibly a fourth bearing southbound on Andrew Young. Yes, he's pulling over. It's a cop. Black Chevrolet Tahoe."

"Roger that, Prosecutor." Snort spoke into the mic as though he were talking through a mouthful of pudding. "We are T minus ninety seconds."

Reed twisted his hand around the familiar grip of the rifle. The rubberized texture rubbed against his palm, loosening his muscles and reminding him of each time he pressed that trigger—the way the weapon lurched into his shoulder, and the puff of red that flashed across his scope before the crosshairs jumped upward. Sitting a thousand yards away and executing judgment on the guilty was the closest feeling to total power.

"Hey, Falcon One," he whispered.

"Yeah, Corporal?"

"That fake leg of yours can still pump a clutch, right?"

Vince snorted. "There's no end to the things this Marine can pump."

"Ooorah!" Falcon Two shouted.

Reed rolled his eyes. "All right. Just making sure. Because if you scratch my car, I'll take it out of your battered jarhead ass."

"I'd welcome you to try, Corporal."

The crosshairs settled over the forty-fifth floor as Reed relaxed his shoulder. The familiar buzz of his cell phone erupted in his pocket, and he pried it out to see the screen illuminated with the all-too-familiar caller ID.

UNKNOWN.

One tap on the green button, and Reed held it to his ear, but he didn't say anything.

"Reed . . . it's three minutes 'til ten. I hope you're not about to disappoint me again."

Reed gasped for air as though he had just climbed a few hundred stairs.

"Listen . . . I'm almost done. Just a couple more minutes."

Salvador grunted. "Ten o'clock, Reed, or Miss Morccelli will be picking her ukulele with three fingers."

The phone clicked off. Reed shoved it back into his pocket and growled into the mic. "Falcon Two, let's go already."

"Just a few more seconds . . . wiring the explosives

now. This is some good junk, Prosecutor. You must have the hookup."

Reed didn't respond. He closed his left eye and focused on the forty-fifth floor. Behind one of the windows, he saw a shadow moving in the darkness. It was graceful and silent. Snort's men may have lost their homes, but they clearly hadn't lost their training.

"All right, Prosecutor. Falcon Two is ready to rock."

"Falcon One?" Reed said.

"Falcon One is in position and ready to roll, Prosecutor."

Reed settled his cheek into the rifle and took one more measured breath. The night fell still and silent, and all noises and distractions were blocked from his mind in this final moment before the storm.

"Falcon Two, execute."

A half second passed, then a loud bang ripped through the quiet night. The window exploded beyond the crosshairs, raining down in deadly shards over the street hundreds of feet below. A body wrapped in dark clothes shot out of the window and fell through empty space, its feet tied by a rope that disappeared back inside the tower. The body soared out from the building with its arms dangling before the cord became taut, and the corpse fell back and slammed against the tower. Crimson blood gushed from the torso, streaming down the building as the arms hung limp next to the glass.

Reed maximized the zoom on the rifle, focusing on the dangling body. He started at the feet, then worked his way down. The legs were covered in dark jeans. The body was wrapped in a dirty denim jacket, now saturated in crimson. Fake blood from the busted reservoir inside the chest streamed over its face. The face was white, distorted by a crushed jaw.

It was a damn-convincing Halloween prop.

Blue lights flashed from the street below. The patrol cars parked on Ellis shot forward, rocketing to the front entrance. Officers piled out of the Impala and Tahoe, while spotlights from all four vehicles blazed over the gaping hole. Reed indulged in a brief smile, enjoying the moment of truth. *It's good to be right.*

"This is Prosecutor. I have four vehicles bearing down on the main entrance. Ten officers closing on your position. Move it, guys."

"Roger that, Prosecutor. We are pulling out."

Reed grinned.

He centered the crosshairs over the main entrance, and they hovered there as cops stormed the door. Dressed in black and clutching assault weapons and tactical shotguns, they were much more heavily armed than your average patrolman. Much too prepared to call it a coincidence.

"Prosecutor, this is Falcon One. I am ready on your mark."

"Wait a moment, Falcon One . . ." Reed looked down at his watch and waited as the seconds ticked by. Ten seconds. Thirty seconds. One minute. He focused on each flash of the digital watch, matching the tempo of time with every pound of his heart, and waiting until the moment felt right.

The tower was bathed in spotlights. Another patrol

car screeched over the pavement from the northeast, a bullhorn squealed, and then a voice barked orders at the tower from somewhere amongst the vehicles. Noise and chaos reigned.

It was time.

"All right, Falcon One. Execute."

A split second passed. Reed swung the crosshairs away from the tower toward the east, and the scope settled over the parking lot that sat between Ellis Street and the Georgia-Pacific Tower. Lights flashed out of the darkness, and an unearthly howl filled his ears. It was the sound of 505 American horses roaring to life.

The Camaro rolled out of the parking lot, then took a gentle turn onto Peachtree Street. Reed imagined he could feel the rumble of the pavement under the uncorked exhaust, shooting up his legs and forcing his body into the rhythm of the engine. He could almost taste the oily flavor of exhaust on the air and feel the familiar leather knob of the shifter under his palm.

The beast slipped down the street at a calm twenty miles per hour, its windows black and its lights dark. Reed traced its path with the scope, zooming out so he could keep the surrounding blocks in view. He bit his lip, held his breath, and then swept the surrounding streets again.

His gaze caught on a glint of steel. He flipped the rifle's safety off and hissed into the mic. "Falcon One, this is Prosecutor. Haul ass."

24

Thunder ripped between the buildings and pounded off the sides of the skyscrapers as the front end of the Camaro lifted off the ground, and the back tires spun against the pavement. A familiar thrill flooded Reed's brain as the car took off, rocketing down Peachtree Street toward Plaza Park. Two more engines, higher-pitched, with shrieking blasts of exhaust, screamed to life fifty yards behind the Camaro. Reed traced Peachtree Street with the crosshairs, back toward the tower, and back toward the police. This was it.

Two suited figures, bent low over Japanese sports bikes, flashed out of a darkened street. They shot through the crowd of cops without so much as a pause, then raced after the Camaro. The air was alive with the roar of the American V-8 and the hellish scream of the bikes.

Reed swung the rifle to the right, following the bikes as they turned into a curve where Peachtree passed the Georgia-Pacific Tower. The motorcycles

vanished out of sight behind the silhouette of the
Residence Inn, and Reed jumped to his feet and
sprinted to the far side of the Equitable Building. He
slid back into a prone position behind the rifle, a
couple of feet from the southern corner of the tower.
Barely a second passed before the Camaro's taillights
flashed across Decatur Street, crossing through the
scope in a millisecond, and then they were gone
again.

"Falcon One, this is Prosecutor. Take a left on Wall
Street, then another left onto Peachtree Center
Avenue."

"Roger that, Prosecutor."

Reed retraced the Camaro's trail until the crosshairs
settled over the sports bikes. The two lean figures bent
over the handlebars with the practiced grace of true
athletes. He could take them out—a clean shot to the
back of each helmet and lay them down in the middle
of Peachtree Street, but that wouldn't bring him any
closer to Banks.

Vince spun the Camaro around the corner onto
Wall Street, then disappeared behind a row of buildings. The bikes followed a hundred yards behind, with
no hint of suspicion or hesitation marking their turns.
The men in hot pursuit of the Camaro were truly
convinced that Reed Montgomery sat behind the wheel
and was putting pedal to the metal to make his escape.

The intersection of Wall Street and Peachtree
Center loomed ahead of the Camaro. A hundred yards.
Then fifty. The car jolted and almost slid into the side-
walk as Vince negotiated a turn. Reed held his breath,

then saw the back tires bite concrete and break the slide at the last moment.

"Falcon Three," Reed whispered. "You ready?"

"I'm all yours, Prosecutor."

Reed laid his finger on the trigger. The first bike flashed into view, crossing the intersection of Peachtree Center and Gilmer Street, right in front of Hurt Park. Reed drew half a breath, the crosshairs froze, and he pressed the trigger.

The front tire of the lead motorcycle exploded. Reed pivoted the crosshairs to the right and pressed the trigger again. The rear tire of the second bike burst. Both bikes slid out of control, slinging their riders into the empty street as the powerful motorcycles spun across the pavement.

Another press of the trigger and a bullet struck home in the left thigh of the first rider. A fourth crack of the rifle blew the second rider's ankle apart, and he convulsed in pain. Both men clawed at their helmets, writhing on the asphalt as blood sprayed from their legs.

"Falcon Three, execute!"

A white utility van roared out of the darkness of Hurt Park, driving against the one-way arrows painted on Gilmer Street. It slid to a stop beside the two fallen men. Reed watched through the scope as a tall man wearing a ski mask jumped out. He stuck a Taser into the rib cage of each man, then dragged their unconscious bodies into the rear of the vehicle. The doors slammed shut, and the van rocketed out of the intersection.

"Prosecutor, this is Falcon Three. Be advised, I have the, um . . . people you wanted."

"Roger that. On my way to the rendezvous. Prosecutor out."

Reed jumped to his feet and ripped the headset off. He ran back to his bags, shoved the radio inside his backpack, and then jerked out the thick bundle of rope. Sparks flashed between the synthetic cord and his damp hands. He ran to the west face of the tower, where a bank of air-conditioning units sat in a six-foot recess on the roof. Reed hurried down the access ladder, then ran to the backside of the humming AC units. His fingers worked in a blur of sweat and rope—a quick flip, and a jerk of both arms to secure the knot. His head pounded again, but the pain was a distant memory overshadowed by the gravity of what came next.

Back on the roof, he flung the rope over the edge and watched it unravel four hundred feet down the side of the tower until it hit the ground. He didn't have time to think about the swimmy feeling in his stomach or the wobble in his knees; everything just blurred together in a series of practiced motions—one foot through the harness, then the next foot. The cinch strap clicked against the buckle as he tightened the harness around his waist, then he slung the backpack over his shoulders, followed by the rifle on the nylon sling. Both were heavy against his back, dragging on his shoulders and making each breath feel short and shallow. Or was that the height?

Reed set the duffle bag beneath the rope, right on

the edge of the rooftop. It provided moderate protection against the sharp edge of the concrete—hardly a professional solution, but hopefully it would suffice. The rope felt heavy as he locked it into his harness, checking each connection and buckle one more time.

Surges of adrenaline drowned out the feeling of absolute terror as he approached the brink of the building. His stomach convulsed, and he fought the overwhelming urge to vomit. Some biological fire alarm wired in his brain erupted in a screaming chorus of warnings. *Get back. Don't do it. Danger! Danger!*

First one foot on the edge, and then the other. Reed's knuckles turned white as he closed his eyes, clutched the rope, and forced himself to lean forward until it became taut. In the distance, he heard police sirens, the blare of the bullhorn, a honking fire truck, boots clapping against the pavement to the pulse of his heart so loud and insistent, he thought it might explode. Bile bubbled up in his throat, but he didn't vomit. He didn't jerk back from the edge.

The white EQUITABLE lights gleamed a couple feet beneath his toes. His hands shook, and he took a long breath between his teeth. It whistled like the blast of the wind in his ears. His knees were locked, and he felt frozen in time, like the moment before the trigger clicked and the rifle cracked.

Go.

The rope slipped through the harness as Reed fell forward. His body rocked over the side of the building until he hung ninety degrees out, suspended by the rope, then continued to plunge. One foot in front of the other, he was a superhero, defiant of gravity or geometry. The rope dangled beneath him, and his heart thundered as his boots pounded down the face of the tower. With each strike of rubber on glass, unshakeable resolve overwhelmed his fear. It was anger now—the kind of anger he felt when he dominated his fears and realized how weak they truly were. He stretched out his legs and leaped forward, allowing fresh yards of rope to hiss through the harness at an ever-increasing speed. He was barely in control, only one false step away from sudden death.

His boots slipped on the slick glass, and Reed tightened his hand on the brake, feeling his shoulders sling forward and his heels fly back. Bile and spit sprayed from his lips as he kicked out at the windows beneath his feet. His toe caught the underside of a windowsill just in time to keep him from plummeting toward the ground in a total free fall. He regained his footing then pushed downward again, rocketing toward the street in a series of hopping leaps. Reed gasped for air, realizing he had been holding his breath since he left the rooftop. Windows and floors flashed past like a blurry slideshow.

The halfway point vanished beneath his feet, and he relaxed his hand on the brake, allowing the rope to slide more quickly through the harness. The brake was hot from the friction, but he didn't let go. He pushed out from the building and released tension, plummeting down another forty feet before his boots struck the glass again.

Almost as quickly as it began, it was over. The

rope ran short, and Reed free-fell the final twelve feet onto the hard sidewalk below. His knees absorbed most of the shock, and he stumbled forward, feeling dizzy and disoriented. The cool night air helped to clear his head as he stumbled away with the rifle bouncing on his shoulders. He tipped his head back to survey the tower, and euphoria overwhelmed his better judgment as he screamed and pumped his fist. "Hell yeah!"

Reed ran up Forsyth Street, pounding the sidewalk in long, smooth strides. He didn't even notice the heavy rifle bouncing on his back or the harness still strapped around his waist. He was consumed by full operator mode and could run through a brick wall if he had to.

Almost there. Just a few more blocks.

Sirens blared from somewhere behind him. The police force would be in a state of total chaos by now. Especially the clean cops, who were unaware of the botched setup that was falling apart and taking their city down with it. Reed hated it when clean cops got mixed up in the dealings of the dirty ones. He could only hope the smoke cleared without any casualties.

Two more blocks passed under his pounding feet. Centennial Olympic Park loomed ahead, and just before it on his right, a small parking lot stretched out between the office buildings. Reed rushed between parked cars, then spotted the utility van parked in the back corner. Its lights were off, but he could tell by the small cloud of vapor building behind the rear tires that the engine was running.

A few quick strides and Reed stopped next to the

driver's door. His legs and chest burned from the exertion.

The door opened, and one of Vince's displaced Marines stepped out. Ellis, a former fuel-truck driver and two-tour veteran, wore a broad smile as though he'd just won a wrestling match.

"They're all yours, Prosecutor. I've got them subdued, but they'll come around soon enough."

Reed offered his hand, his chest still heaving. "Thank you. I owe you guys . . . big time."

Ellis shrugged. "Don't worry about it. We don't have a lot to lose. It felt good to have some excitement for a change."

"It still means a lot. Next Monday afternoon, you'll find a man sitting on the park bench where I found Vince tonight. He'll leave a suitcase and walk away. Split it up with the guys."

Reed handed him a black card with a ten-digit number printed on one side in silver ink. The rest of the card was blank.

"This is me. I'm one call away."

Ellis offered a casual salute. "Good luck, Prosecutor. Give 'em hell."

As the battered Marine disappeared around the corner, Reed shoved his gear into the van and then piled in after it. Hell was a good word for what lay ahead.

25

The van coughed and lurched forward. Reed looked over his shoulder to see the motorcycle riders laid out in the rear, unconscious amid shelves of electrical wire and fallen hand tools. The van belonged to a local electrical contractor, and Reed stole it from their service lot an hour before breaching the Equitable building. Vince would leave the Camaro at a prearranged drop point, but for now, the van would be less conspicuous.

Once again, the phone buzzed in Reed's pocket, but this time he didn't bother to check the caller ID.

"What's up, creep?"

Salvador's smooth voice was taut with anger. "Reed, you just made a very costly mistake."

"Help me out here, Sal. Was it a mistake to kick your goons in the nuts, or to evade your underhanded attempt to frame me? It's difficult to keep up with your games."

Short, hissing breaths blasted through the speaker. "All right. If that's how you want it, cut off her hand!"

"You're not good at blackmail, are you?"

The line fell silent. Salvador's tense breathing paused.

"Take notes, Sal. The first rule of blackmail: Never threaten a person you can't control."

"You think I'm scared of you, Montgomery?" Salvador's voice snapped like a bullwhip.

"Apparently not. But you're about to be."

"Listen, you shit. I'm about to filet this girl like—"

Reed hung up and tossed the phone into the passenger's seat. It buzzed again, but Reed ignored it. He turned off the highway and drove through the quiet streets of a neighborhood, taking increasingly more isolated streets until he found a long, desolate road leading out toward a garbage dump. Dust fogged the air around him as he bounced over potholes and swerved around deep ruts, driving another three miles before stopping in front of the dump's main entrance. A single streetlight buzzed over the gate, washing the chain link fence in a pool of orange warmth. The motor died, and the empty space around the landfill became still. Reed surveyed his surroundings for any sign of electronic surveillance, but he saw none. This far from the city, isolation ruled.

Dried mud crunched under his feet next to the van, and the air was thick with the smog of rotting garbage and pervasive diesel fumes. The motorcyclists groaned in agony as Reed jerked them through the back door and allowed them to collapse onto the ground. A few layers of duct tape bound their hands and sealed their wounds, moderating the flow of blood. Pale faces flooded with fear were framed by small features and blonde hair. European, clearly, and probably from east of Germany. One of the old Com-Bloc nations, maybe. Desperate men so long lost in the mire of the criminal underworld that they wouldn't be recognized by their own mothers. Reed knew the type.

Quick jabs to the gunshot wounds with the toe of his boot brought both men back to full consciousness. Groans turned to screams, and they began to kick. Reed dealt each a swift blow to the jaw, slamming their heads back against the rear of the van, then he squatted in front of them and drew the Glock.

"I haven't got a lot of time. Who do you work for, and where is Banks Morccelli?"

"To hell with you, man."

The accent was exactly as Reed suspected—thick, Eastern European, laden with heavy L's and rolled R's.

Reed laid the muzzle of the pistol against the man's left kneecap and pressed the trigger. Blood exploded from the leather pants, and the man screamed and jerked away, slamming his head into the back of the van. A waterfall of agony streamed from his eyes, drawing wavering lines through the dirt on his cheeks.

"I think I have your attention." Reed's tone remained level and focused. "Whoever talks first gets to live. Who do you work for?"

The men glared at him in defiant silence, and the

one on the left groaned and shook in pain, but still didn't speak.

"Damn you people. You're only hurting yourself." Reed holstered the pistol and walked around to the side of the van. He dug through the pile of tools until he located a pair of electrician's cable-cutters—thick, heavy-duty pliers with rusted handles. He returned to the rear of the van and placed the righthand man's index finger between the cutting jaws of the pliers.

"What the—"

The landfill echoed with agonized screams as Reed clamped down on the pliers. Bone was no match for his grip.

"Who do you work for?"

His victim shook like a tree in a hurricane, then beat his head against the back of the van, leaving smears of blood on the dusty white paint. Reed cocked back his fist and dealt him a swift blow to the jaw with the pliers. Bone cracked. Reed struck again, and the man on the left cursed in protest. Reed switched fire and beat him over the face, collapsing his nose.

"Do you know what they call me?" Reed asked. "They call me The Prosecutor. Because when I've got a job, I prosecute the hell out of it until I get the results I want. You two dirtbags made a huge mistake getting in my way."

Reed wiped his forehead. His stomach was ready to bust each time he looked down at his bloody handi-work, but the resolve in his mind was as inflexible as iron.

"One of you has a chance to walk away. Who do you work for?"

The men sat trembling, blood puddling on the ground around them. Reed waited. Sometimes the fear itself was more powerful than waves of pain.

The man on the right spoke first. "I do not know name. He—"

"Shut up!" His partner sank his teeth into the man's shoulder.

Reed snatched the pistol from his belt and fired twice. Blood sprayed across the rear door of the van. The body toppled to the ground.

"Continue." Reed's voice was dull and emotionless.

"I do not know him! We get contract, just like you. He tell us police will arrest you. We stop you if you try to escape. This is all, I swear!"

Reed holstered the gun and squatted in front of him, toying with the pliers.

"How were you paid?"

"Cash. American dollars."

"Who paid you?"

"Nobody. We get job through Swiss broker. They call him Cedric. We were told to pick up the cash in locker at train station. This was all!"

"You're lying." Reed lifted the pliers.

"No! Okay. Okay. We work for him before. The man in Georgia. I do not know his name."

"Salvador? Is he called Salvador?"

"Salvador? No. He is English."

"English?" Reed cocked his head. "You mean he's white?"

"I don't know!" He looked away and slammed his head into the van again.

Reed grabbed him by the collar and jerked him forward, forcing him to meet his gaze.

"What did you do?"

Breath whistled between his bloody teeth. His eyes reminded Reed of the way pupils looked after being dilated at the optometrist—wide, vacant, and unnatural.

"There was girl. I do not know who. He wanted her taken."

"Describe her."

Again, he tried to look away, but Reed dropped the pliers and sent his fist crashing directly below his victim's left eye. Knuckles met flesh with all the vengeance and power of the practiced blows back at the cabin. Once, then twice, then came the third stroke, driving the man's head into the rear of the van.

Reed leaned closer and screamed into this ear. "What did she look like?"

The man sobbed. "Blonde. Pretty. Young twenties."

"Where did you take her?"

"Train! Train place. I do not know name! No trains come. Only empty."

Reed shook him by the collar then raised his fist again. "Abandoned? It's abandoned?"

"Yes! Is abandoned."

"In the city?"

"Yes . . . yes. In the city."

Reed knew the location. It was the last place anyone would look—empty and isolated, with plenty of places to hide a kidnapped woman. He tossed the pliers into his left hand and drew the pistol.

The prisoner stared down the muzzle.

"No! You said if I talk, I live!"

Reed's eyes stung, and he swallowed hard. "I did, and you would have. But you touched Banks. I'm sorry."

The pistol cracked, and the man fell to the ground. Reed's arms trembled, his vision fogged, and the world tipped under his feet as he stepped away from the bodies and leaned against the van. Nausea and vertigo overwhelmed him, washing down his body like a tidal wave of illness. Vomit hurtled through his throat and splashed over his boots.

God, forgive me.

The bodies crumpled over each other in the back of the van. Reed tossed the pliers inside, then shut the door and kicked dirt over the pools of blood under his feet. He drove back to the four-lane highway and turned east. The pavement drummed under the cheap tires, and occasional cars flashed past in the oncoming lanes. Reed's head spun, but he forced back the feelings of confused remorse. There was no time to feel sorry for the guilty.

He pulled the van into a dark, abandoned shopping mall southeast of town. Broken and abandoned shopping carts sat at random throughout the lot, while paper bags and bits of trash skipped over the pavement. Reed parked behind the main building and grabbed his gear. After digging through one of the dead man's pockets, he located a cell phone. It was locked but still allowed him to dial 911.

"What's your emergency?"

The sleeve of his jacket tasted bitter as he pressed it against his lips and spoke in a dull monotone. "You'll find Senator Holiday in a trailer off of Grimley Road. Bring medical."

Reed hung up before the operator could respond, and he threw the cell into the back of the van. He drew the Glock and bent over under the rear bumper. One shot to the bottom of the plastic gas tank resulted in a stream of fuel gushing over the pavement. The gasoline gurgled and splashed over the asphalt and tires, and filled the air with the thick aroma of petrol. He stepped back a few feet, holstered the gun, and lit a cigarette. His fingers trembled as he lifted it to his lips, but the nicotine brought relief to his strained nerves. His joints loosened, and he relished the fog that consumed his brain—not really a distraction, and barely a shield. It was a filter that blocked out the worst of the last hour, clearing his thoughts of the screams and carnage.

What have I become?

Reed flipped the smoke beneath the van. The gas exploded into a red-hot ball of fire, lifting the rear tires an inch off the ground before consuming the vehicle in flames. They were hot on his face, singeing his skin like a summer sun. Reed turned away.

The Camaro sat in the shadows, melting into the darkness like a ghost. He opened the trunk and deposited the rifle and gear, then slid into the driver's seat. Pain ripped through his legs and torso, reminding him that his adrenaline high was receding. There was nothing he could do about that. There would be time for painkillers and whiskey later.

Reed slammed the car into gear and took the on-ramp onto I-24 East. He planted his foot into the accelerator and listened to the roar of the wind and motor meld together in a bellow of hellish defiance that matched the rage building in the back of his mind.

It was time to finish this.

The miles passed under the belly of the Camaro in a dark blur. Reed circumvented the heart of the city, knowing it would still be hot with police activity. There was almost certainly an APB on the Camaro, which left him only a few hours before the investigative net of the Atlanta PD tightened too much for him to enter the city at all. By sunrise, both the car and its driver would need to be far away.

After taking the bypass around the southern side of the city, Reed turned north along State Highway 23 through Thomasville. His heart rate quickened as he closed in on East Atlanta. A lot of railroads cut between the streets and houses, and there were plenty of rail yards, also. Several of those were abandoned, the skeletons of an industrial age now passed. But when the tortured goon mentioned an empty rail yard where Salvador held Banks, only one place came to mind.

Pratt-Pullman Yard.

The streets around the Camaro grew darker and

more desolate. Old houses with faded and peeling paint lined the sidewalks, many of them abandoned with shattered windows and boarded-up doors. Giant oak trees leaned over the streets with wiry branches hovering over rotting rooftops. Many of these trees remembered the Civil War; they were the survivors of the flames that consumed Atlanta, and they felt unwelcoming to Reed's violent intrusion, as though this place had seen enough of conflict and only wanted to sleep.

Reed stopped the car where he could see the rusty rooftops of the train yard a few hundred yards ahead. Just beyond it, MARTA's Blue Line ripped through the neighborhood and toward the east, lit by soft streetlights and red track lamps. Everything was unmoving and reserved, as though the trees and the darkness housed a terrible secret. There was an unnatural calm that promised awful things to anyone who broke it. Could that secret be Banks?

The body armor was heavy and restrictive as Reed pulled it on. He didn't tighten the straps as much this time, but he tucked an extra magazine into the elastic straps of the chest plate. The KRISS Vector, fully loaded, hung from a single-point sling around his neck. Half-dry blood stuck to his hands and forearms, and it was splattered over his pants and covered his shoes.

Reed slammed the trunk closed and stepped around to the side door of the Camaro. For the first time since hanging up on the unknown caller three hours before, he looked down at his phone. There were four missed calls, all from the same number. Reed hit redial.

The voice that answered was the furthest thing from the calm and controlled speaker of the last twenty-four hours. Salvador was consumed by anger, and his South American snarl muddled the clarity of his words, converting them into a stream of verbal vomit.

"It's too late, Montgomery. We've killed her!"

Reed forced himself to remain calm. "If that were true, you wouldn't have answered."

A crashing sound erupted from over the phone. "I'm going to rip her limb from limb!"

"Shut up." Reed's patience snapped like a strained rubber band. "I'm giving you one chance to walk away. Leave Banks, and get out while you're still alive."

"I'm not scared of you, Reed! You want her? Come get her!"

Reed hung up and pulled the charging handle of the submachine gun. The heavy bolt cycled back and rammed a fresh round into the chamber. His body was tense and charged, his mind sharpened, and he focused on the metal building rising over the shingle roofs three hundred yards away. The battered tin was painted with graffiti and full of holes, and the moonlight illuminated Pratt-Pullman as though it were a stage. Reed thought about the way Banks laughed and the overwhelming obsession he felt the second her lips touched his. The sound of her fingers strumming the ukulele, looking out over Atlanta. A city she loved. A place she called home.

Reed broke into a run toward the train yard.

27

Banks couldn't see. Her head was numb, and her eyes stung like they were filled with pepper juice. She knew there was some type of sedative in her veins, and it caused her mind to work in slow motion, as though each thought was its own private marathon. She blinked and tried to focus on tangible concepts, things she could work with, information that was relevant.

Her hands were tied behind her back and around the chair. She could work with that. What kind of bonds were they? Hard and narrow. Cable ties, maybe? Her feet were also bound, locked to the chair's legs with more cables. A dirty cloth that tasted like gasoline filled her mouth.

Her heart pounded like a war drum. Even through the drugs, the fear was palpable, building into a driving force that urged her to embrace the panic and descend into mental anarchy. She tried to identify her last clear memory, but everything was fuzzy. Was she in the Beetle or just near it? No, she wasn't in it. She was walking toward it. In a parking lot? Yes, it was a parking lot. There was a shopping bag in her hand. New socks and a bag of potato chips. That detail rang ironically clear in her crowded mind.

She remembered a split second of fear before the world erupted into chaos. There were men . . . two of them. Maybe more. They jumped from the side of a van and ran toward her. She fumbled with her purse, reaching for the Smith & Wesson 637 buried inside, and she struggled with the holster. The hammer spur caught on the inside of the bag, and panic overwhelmed her mind.

And then there was blackness. Had they hit her? Her head didn't hurt, but her neck throbbed.

Banks sank her teeth into the towel and pulled at the bonds. Nothing loosened. She tried to scream past the wadded cloth in her mouth, but the muted moan sounded more like a grunt than a cry for help.

Light flooded her face, and she blinked and tried to focus through her blurred vision and numb mind. She could see a door on the far side of the room, and two men stepped in. They moved in a blur of black clothes and stomping boots, lifted the chair off the floor, and carried her across the room.

A third man, short with dark skin, appeared and snapped angry commands at the others. "Hurry! Put her on the train. If you don't hear from me in ten minutes, go through with it."

Banks kicked against the chair, and a gloved fist

slammed into her cheekbone. She tried to scream, but everything hurt. Panic surged through her mind, but this time it was accompanied by rage.

Another fist to her temple and she choked and slumped forward. The world spun.

Reed held the submachine gun to his chest and leaned low as he ran northward along Rogers Street. Everything was deathly silent. He checked the rifle for the third time as Toomer Elementary School loomed to his right. The school was dark and the parking lot empty. On the far side of the schoolyard a row of trees blocked the south edge of Pullman Yard. Reed jogged across the lot and slipped into the trees, and his boots fell in soft thumps on the leaf-covered ground.

He ducked under a limb and paused at the edge of the tree line. The bulk of Pratt-Pullman stood directly ahead in a cluster of large warehouse buildings. The space between consisted of a mostly empty field with a few abandoned structures and shallow ditches. To his right, the trees became thicker and looped their way along the east side of the field and toward the warehouses. The foliage was dense and tangled, ensuring a difficult and time-consuming approach. The alternative, however, would be to make a direct dash across an exposed three-hundred-yard stretch.

He opted for the trees and turned right, working his way through the brush for fifty yards before turning north and moving along the east edge of the field. The forest floor was littered with dry sticks and shallow holes, making it difficult to walk without sounding like an army of squirrels bouncing through the leaves. Reed bent under the low-hanging limbs and held the gun just under his line of sight, his finger extended over the trigger guard. Each breath was shallow. Every movement charged with nervous excitement.

As he approached the warehouses, the trees began to thin, and standing just twenty yards from the tree line was the first of the metal structures. They consisted of four narrow buildings, with sloping tin roofs, built directly next to each other. The walls were rusted and full of wide holes, exposing nothing but darkness on the other side. Reed slipped up next to the first structure and swept the muzzle of the rifle over the landscape around it. There were no signs of life. Moonlight played hide-and-seek with the shadows as the trees swayed in the wind. In the distance, an owl hooted, and some kind of nocturnal rodent bounced through the leaves. Reed's arm trembled with tension.

Thirty yards across a small field littered with trailer parts and manufacturing paraphernalia stood the train yard's primary structure. Over a hundred yards long, it dominated the field in rusty red—a relic of another era. The eastern end of the building was buried in the trees, with foliage and kudzu vines growing over the side and onto the roof, threatening to consume the building back into the belly of nature. The southern wall faced Reed with a series of twelve garage-style doors. Half of them hung open, gaping like the hungry mouths of a sleeping beast. Windows ran along the sloping rooftop, and most of them were busted out, leaving shards of dirty glass glistening in the moonlight. Graffiti covered every exposed inch of the building, blasted in gaudy shades of spray paint over the metal and brick. Nothing about the shadowy structure was hospitable. Reed realized there would be no chance of breaching it without exposing himself. Once inside, it would be dark. The floor could be concrete, strewn with machinery and sections of railroad iron. Worse still, the floor might be constructed of rotting wood ready to give way under the slightest provocation. He understood why Salvador chose this spot. It wasn't isolated or hidden or even defensible, but it was utterly impossible to approach without complete exposure.

Reed disengaged the safety and laid his finger over the trigger. He cast a wary look around the open field, checking for any new signs of surveillance or defense. Then he launched himself out of the trees and toward the building.

Three strides into the field and one leap over a ditch. That was as far as Reed made it before the first gunshots shattered the stillness. They were small-caliber, fully automatic, and blazing from one of the windows near the roofline. The ground exploded around his feet, sending rocks blasting into the air as though a land mine had detonated. Reed ducked and dashed to the left, and the gunfire continued, spraying the field with a deluge of lead.

It must be some kind of com-block submachine gun, inaccurate beyond fifty or sixty yards, clapping and thundering like some kind of deranged DJ hooked on a bass loop. Reed raised the KRISS and flipped the thumb switch to fully automatic, then pressed the trigger. The gun rattled like a firecracker, dumping twenty-five rounds of .45 ACP slugs into the building at random. The gunshots from the warehouse ceased, and Reed accelerated toward the building. He dropped the empty magazine and slammed a new one into the mag well, then smacked the bolt release with the heel of his left hand. Every sound rang in his head, pounding and echoing as though individually amplified. Reed skidded to a halt next to one of the gaping garage doors, pulled the gun into his shoulder, and ducked through the door. The inside of the warehouse stretched out before him, lit by the moon shining through the holes in the roof. As soon as his foot crossed the threshold, the gunfire resumed. He pivoted toward the sound and raised the KRISS. Muzzle flash blazed from a catwalk a few dozen yards away, suspended high above the concrete floor. Reed aligned the red dot over the spot and pressed the trigger twice. Something blunt struck his left calf, tearing through his pants like a red-hot spike. Reed grunted and fell sideways to the floor, still firing at the catwalk. The warehouse thundered with the sound of gunfire, reverberating off the tin walls. Somebody screamed, and a body hit the floor with a meaty crash. More gunfire erupted from the far end of the warehouse, ripping through the open space toward Reed.

He rolled to the left and forced himself to his feet. Sticky hot blood streamed down his left leg and over his boot as he pivoted toward the gunfire and pressed the trigger. Before he could fire again, something struck his right shoulder, and he collapsed to the ground. A tall man wielding a nightstick loomed over his head, and Reed rolled to his right just in time to dodge a sweeping blow from the baton. A boot landed on his knee and pressed down with over two hundred pounds of force. Reed jerked his leg free, then jammed his left boot into his attacker's shin. The submachine gun lay tangled in the sling under his arm. Reed grabbed the Glock instead and fired twice at the man's face. The attacker clattered to the ground. Reed fought his way to his feet, and the world turned as though he were on a carnival ride and being slung in and out while being forced to listen to a drumbeat of hell the whole time.

He holstered the Glock and lifted the submachine gun. A quick sweep of the warehouse revealed two bodies lying on the ground thirty yards away. One of them writhed in pain, clutching his stomach as blood puddled around him. The other lay still.

Reed conducted two more sweeps of the building, ensuring that no blind spots might hide additional assailants, then broke into a run toward the wounded man on the floor. The gunman blurred out of focus, fading in and out of a red mist. Reed kicked him in the ribs.

"Where is she?" he screamed.

The gunman's eyes narrowed. Reed shoved his heel into the bullet wound, pressing until the building echoed with screams of agony.

Reed jammed the muzzle of the gun into the man's right eye socket and screamed again.

"*Where is she?*"

"Do it."

A calm voice with a thick, South American accent rang out from behind him. Reed spun on his heel and raised the submachine gun. The man standing twenty yards away was framed by the shadows. He was barely five feet tall, dressed in a heavy overcoat and fedora, with his hands jammed into his pockets.

Reed laid his finger over the trigger. "Game's up, Sal. Where is she?"

Salvador's laugh rumbled and then thundered from his throat. It was a full, gleeful sound of triumph. The blaze in his eyes intensified, as though he didn't control his own reactions—as though he were the slave of an invisible drug.

"Put down the gun, Reed. This is checkmate."

A crimson flash caught Reed's eye, and he looked down, relaxing his trigger finger as he did. The red dot that hovered over his chest twitched back and forth, forming X patterns over his heart. Reed traced the laser sight up and onto the roof of the building where an unseen shooter lay in overwatch—his sights fixed on Reed.

"You could have made it simple, Reed," Salvador said. "But honestly, we thought you'd respond this way. It's why we had a backup plan."

Reed lowered the gun and ran his tongue over dry and cracked lips. The unbendable iron in his mind returned, bringing control back to his anger.

"Whoever you are, you're in way over your head," Reed snapped. "When you screw with me, you screw with my company. It's not a game you can win."

"*Your* company?" Salvador tilted his head. "Don't you mean Oliver's company?"

A knife of uncertainty sliced through his chest. Then he heard a familiar footfall clicking on the concrete. The moonlight cut through the roof overhead, illuminating the new figure emerging from the shadows. He was tall, slender, and balding, with a thin grey beard.

The gun trembled in Reed's damp fingers as his heart thundered.

"*Oliver*?"

Oliver Enfield shoved his hands into his pockets and stepped beside Salvador. His battered old face was set in hard lines, and his brow furrowed into a stony frown—every inch of him looked the part of a disgusted killer.

"I gave you a chance, Reed." Oliver's voice rumbled like distant thunder. "This wasn't my first choice. I would have given you the world, and all you wanted was to walk."

The shock gave way to untethered rage, and Reed remembered the words of the bloodied biker at the landfill—how he had called his employer "English." He didn't mean white. He meant British. He meant Oliver Enfield.

"Thirty kills," Reed screamed. "That was the deal. Then I'm free!"

"That's right, Reed. Free to continue working for my company as long as you draw breath."

"So, it's all a racket." Reed spat the words as though they were venom. It was all he could do not to sling himself forward and tear Oliver's throat out, even as the red dot continued to dance over his chest.

"No, Reed. It's a company. A company you work for until you die. And you had that chance. You could have climbed as high as you wanted. Maybe one day, you would have taken my place. *The Prosecutor,* my brightest, most ruthless killer. But instead, you threw that back in my face. You ungrateful, whiny child!"

"You kidnapped Banks. You killed Brent. You set me up from day one!"

"No." Oliver shook his head. "The Holiday hit was a legitimate job, a contract made for the legitimate people that Mr. Salvador works for. You were the one who ruined a good thing. Do you think I could just let you walk away? Kill thirty people and then just leave with all you know and all you've seen? Of course not. So, Mr. Salvador and I decided to kill two birds with one stone: Senator Holiday . . . and you."

Reed snorted. "Don't kid yourself, Oliver. After your man guns me down, your whole world is going to cave in. Didn't you think I'd hedge my bets? I've dirt on you, stored away someplace where the FBI will find it. Enough to send you straight to death row for Holiday's death."

It was a bluff, all of it. Reed was a killer, not a chess master. He never thought to question Oliver, and now he was going to die for it.

Oliver stood in silence, his hands still jammed into his pockets. The groans of the wounded man had faded, and even the wind outside the warehouse died down. Oliver stepped forward, his expensive leather shoes tapping the concrete with grace and precision. He stopped in front of Reed, faced him eye to eye, then calmly put one hand on his shoulder and smiled.

"You're the perfect killer, Reed. Cold. Brutal. Nothing to lose. You've only got one problem: You can't appreciate the shades of grey—the cunning of an old man. Holiday isn't dead—I know that. But I'm not going to kill you. I could have done that from day one, but then I'd have to explain to the whole company that I'm not a ruthless backstabber. How can I expect to maintain the trust and effort of my contractors if I gun down their colleagues? It's not good for morale. So no, I've got other plans for you. I'm going to let *you* clean this up."

Oliver squeezed his shoulder and stared at Reed, cold and emotionless. The smile faded, leaving nothing but the ashen glare of a relentless monster. Oliver slapped him on the shoulder, jammed his hands back into his pockets, then turned and jerked his head at Salvador as he walked toward the door.

"Enjoy prison, Reed. You might recall that I have a lot of influence when it comes to incarceration. Correctional facilities are funny places full of all kinds of people waiting to throttle a man in his sleep." Oliver laughed. "None of my other contractors could blame me for that, could they?"

Police sirens rang in the distance, blending with the thunder of a chopper from someplace overhead. The Atlanta PD was closing in on the train yard like a pack of bloodhounds eager to sink their teeth into the red-handed killer standing inside. Reed remained silent as Oliver stopped at the door and then twisted his neck. It popped like a gunshot.

Reed spoke calmly, with no hint of malice. "I'll take you down with me." It was a promise.

Oliver glanced back at Reed. His smile was wide this time, exposing a row of perfect teeth. "Wanna bet?"

A truck roared to life outside, and the gunman in the shadows lifted his rifle and vanished behind Oliver and Salvador through the doorway. The police sirens screamed from somewhere in the east, bearing down on the warehouse. Tires spun, and rocks clanged against the building as Reed ran to the door, raising his gun and searching for a target. But the truck had already disappeared around the corner; its fading taillights passed out of view and into a hidden path between the trees.

Reed coughed on the dust and started to run, but then he heard the screech of metal on metal, the whistle of air snapping around each car, and the clack of wheels rattling on a train track. By themselves the sounds heralded nothing more than the routine passing of the nearby MARTA train, but then he heard the scream—ripping and unearthly.

He knew that voice; he would've recognized it anywhere.

Reed bolted toward the far end of the warehouse, slid through a gap in the tin, and ran. Forty yards away, he saw it: MARTA's Blue Line train rocketing out of Edgewood Station toward Indian Creek. The lights on the train flashed, and passengers locked inside the row of cars pounded against the windows and clawed at the sliding doors. The train hadn't stopped at Edgewood. It barreled down the track at full speed, sparks flying from the wheels. The windshield of the driver's booth was shattered, with blood sprayed against the glass, and there, handcuffed to the doorframe, was Banks.

Reed's heart slammed into his throat, and in the

split second it took to recognize Banks, it all made sense. *Checkmate*—Oliver's final ploy to frame Reed and send him back to prison, there to be executed at the hands of an endless network of criminal butchers. It was the ultimate maneuver. Even if Reed ran for the hills, everything would be hung on him now. Oliver would feed the FBI and the media whatever they needed to pin the carnage on Reed and run him to ground, with no risk of anything undermining the stability of the company.

Reed could drag it out, of course. He could hide and manipulate, and raise hell for Oliver. Do everything he could to burn the world down. That was why they handcuffed Banks to the front of the train—so Reed never had the option to run.

The roar of the train pounded in his head, and every other noise and stimulant faded away as he ran toward the track, watching Banks flash past. Her blonde hair was torn by the wind, and her screams were drowned out by the train.

Reed slid to a stop at the chainlink fence that barred his path to the rail line, watching as the last car flashed past. He knew the train wouldn't stop. All MARTA cars were fitted with automatic braking systems to prevent derailing in an emergency, but Oliver would have disabled them. Nothing would keep the train from hurtling the last seven miles to the track terminus, there to explode in a wreckage of twisted metal and shattered bodies.

He dashed back toward the warehouse, tripping over a piece of railroad track along the way. His right leg ignited in pain, and thick blood oozed over his cargo pants. There were three dead men inside the warehouse, and not all of them could have arrived in Oliver's truck. There must've been another vehicle.

Think.

Reed charged through the rail yard, searching behind stacks of machinery and rotting railroad timbers. Entire portions of the yard were consumed by vines and undergrowth, slowly dying as winter approached. Dry dirt crumbling under his boots filled the air around him with a red cloud. Reed clawed the flashlight from his belt and clicked it on. He saw footprints, ruts, shallow ditches, and then the tracks. They crisscrossed the thin dirt, then disappeared into one of the sheds. A red taillight glimmered through the holes in the tin, reflecting against the powerful LED.

He dashed back into the big warehouse, slid to his knees next to the fallen gunman, and ripped through his pockets. There was a watch, a knife, and a wad of dirty cash. And then he found the keys.

Reed's left leg was numb as he pulled himself back to his feet and ran. The earth rang with dull thuds as his boots struck the packed dust. He couldn't hear the train anymore, and police sirens screamed down Rogers Street only a hundred yards away.

Reed slung his leg over the big Japanese sports bike, jammed the key into the ignition, clamped his hand down on the clutch, and kicked the starter. The engine roared to life with a devilish scream. The rear tire spun on dry concrete, and Reed flashed out of the shed as police cars skidded into the empty lot between the buildings. Floodlights blinded him, and somebody screamed for him to stop. A pistol popped, followed by rifle shots. Reed gunned the engine, and the front tire lifted off the ground. He clung to the bike as the KRISS bounced on his back, riding on the ends of the sling.

He skidded around the corner of the building and shot onto Rogers Street. The bike shook as he slammed it into second gear and swerved around a black SUV loaded with SWAT responders. Everybody shouted at him to stop, and a bullhorn blared. The road opened in front of the bike, and houses flashed past, followed by Toomer Elementary. He leaned into a sharp left turn onto Hosea L Williams Drive and twisted the grip to max throttle.

30

R eed gunned the bike past ninety miles an hour as he rocketed through subdivisions and small shopping strips. MARTA's Blue Line led through the East Lake Station before diving beneath Decatur. On the far side of the city, Avondale was the first place the train resurfaced and traveled above ground. Reed remembered a low bridge that crossed over the tracks just past the station. If he could get to that bridge before the train, he might have a chance of stopping it.

He hit the brakes and planted his boot on the ground, sliding into a left turn before he downshifted and hit the throttle again. As the motor whined and the bike surged northward onto Howard Street, time stood still.

The trees and the houses under the night sky faded around him, and he could feel the hot California breeze on his face. He heard the thunder of his old 1992 Suzuki, smelled the salt wind blowing off the Pacific coast, and felt the surge of panicked adrenaline as a squad car closed in on his tail. He remembered the rush of blind recklessness as he gunned the big bike and pulled away from the cop. The world and all of its problems were no longer concerns. The only thing that mattered was clearing the next block, sliding through the next traffic light, and vanishing back into the sweet freedom of south Los Angeles.

Reed refocused on the dark street and hooked a right onto College Avenue North East. There were no traffic lights and no stop signs. The avenue opened up as far as he could see, disappearing into the darkness toward Decatur. Reed shifted up and wound the engine out. As the RPM meter rose, the speedometer passed one hundred miles an hour. The neighborhood faded into the dark corners of his vision, and the street became a grey tunnel leading forward between the trees. Lights flashed over either shoulder as Decatur rocketed into view, and the speedometer hit one-forty as the RPM meter hovered close to redline. Reed leaned forward and pressed his body into the bike. The wind blasted his face, almost blinding him as the bike bounced over the slight imperfections in the road.

East Lake Station passed on his left, and there was no sign of the train. He pressed the throttle harder, but the big Japanese engine was pushed to its max. The train tracks on his left vanished into the ground as MARTA's Blue Line dove under the city toward Decatur Station. There was a chance that MARTA headquarters had been able to apply the brakes remotely. Even now, the train might be screeching to a stop deep beneath the pavement, but Reed couldn't take that chance.

College Avenue stretched out perfectly straight in front of him for miles. The train would make seventy miles an hour under full speed, and the bike was locked at a hard one-forty.

Maybe enough.

Seconds passed. Avondale Station was five hundred yards ahead, and just to his left, the Blue Line rose out of the tunnel and back to ground level. Reed's heart skipped a beat as he saw the train flash out of the darkness, still flying eastward at full speed. He caught sight of Banks clinging to the front of the train, her hair whipping as the car careened forward. Her left foot had been knocked off the front bumper, and she clung to the front door handle as one leg dangled inches above the tracks.

Reed looked forward just in time to swerve and miss an oncoming truck, then he leaned to the right and applied the brake as he rounded a gentle curve on College Avenue. Avondale Station flashed past on his left, and he could hear the clacking roar of the train just over his left shoulder, a hundred yards behind him. A large four-way intersection lay directly ahead, connecting College Avenue with Sam's Crossing. The bridge that spanned the Blue Line waited there.

Reed released pressure on the throttle and leaned to the left, then slammed on the brake. The bike shuddered and slid, and he struggled to keep it upright as the g-force almost slung him off the seat. The intersection flashed around him, and he turned the bike left on Sam's Crossing and clamped down on the brake again. The motorcycle slid onto the bridge, and he saw Avondale Station beneath him, a hundred yards west. The headlights of the train flashed into view, coming out of the station and rocketing toward the bridge.

The bike screeched to a halt and slammed down on its side. Reed screamed in pain and fought to free his leg from underneath the piping-hot engine block. He heard the train crashing along the track as it passed beneath the bridge. He jerked his leg free, tearing fabric and flesh against the side of the bike, and leaving the air reeking with burning rubber and singed cloth.

Reed jumped to his feet and limped to the edge of the bridge. He didn't have time to think. The last car passed under the bridge, and Reed grabbed the guard rail and flipped his legs over. The open air whistled past his ears as he free-fell ten feet. His boots slammed into the metal roof of the last car, his legs slipped from under him, and he landed on his side, sliding backward over the slick sheet metal toward the rear of the car. Reed shouted and grabbed at the ridges in the metal, clawing for anything to hold onto.

His fingers caught on a ridge in the roof, slowing him down just enough to keep him from flying off the side. The wind roared in his ears as the car rose and fell beneath him, clacking against the metal rails. His legs spun off the roof, hanging in midair before slamming down against the side of the car. Reed clawed his way forward, and a fingernail split. With a Herculean effort, he slung his left leg up and over, and pulled himself back onto the roof. He lay five feet from the tail of the train, and began to claw his way toward the rear emergency door.

Reed twisted and grabbed the rear rim of the roof, then pulled himself toward it. The train rattled over a joint in the track, and he looked forward just in time to plant his face against the metal. A bridge flashed overhead, inches above his shoulder blades. He looked up again toward the front of the train and felt the cold claw of fear sink into his heart. Another tunnel was rapidly approaching, and he could already tell there wasn't enough clearance for a man to lie on top of the car.

Reed grabbed the top rim of the train and slung his legs over the edge, free-falling toward the track. His knees slammed into the rear of the car as his full weight descended on his fingers, and he kicked out with his feet, fighting for any hint of a purchase. The rifle sling caught on the top of the emergency doorframe, tying him to the rear of the train and tightening around his neck, choking him as the train rocketed into the tunnel. He jerked at the sling, but it wouldn't tear free. Reaching down, he grabbed the butt of the rifle and pressed the quick-release. The sling snapped free and slid around his neck just as his boots caught the edge of what must have been the rear bumper. The rifle dangled against the side of the train, then the sling slipped free of the doorframe and the gun disappeared into the darkness.

Reed gasped for air and let go of the roof with his right hand. He grabbed the exterior handle of the emergency door and jerked it up. The door opened, and he shoved his right foot into the gap before sliding to the right, allowing the door to swing open. He let go of the roof and slung himself inside the train. The door slammed shut behind him, and for a moment, everything was shockingly still.

His head spun as he looked up to see terrified commuters standing at the front of the car, staring back at him with wild eyes.

Reed clawed his way to his feet and stumbled forward, shouting over the clacking rattle of the train.

"Get to the back! Hold on to something. Help the others!"

No one responded. Reed raised his voice and pointed to the rear of the car. "Stand in the back! We're going to crash! Grab the rails!"

He shoved past the remaining commuters and to the front of the car. The tunnel disappeared around him as he jerked open the emergency door at the front of the car and stepped out onto the coupling between the cars. As he burst through the next door, he was already shouting.

"Go to the rear car! We're going to crash! Hold on to something!"

The commuters screamed and fought their way past him.

Reed pushed ahead and ran through the next two cars, shouting at the passengers and waving toward the rear of the train.

"Move now! Get to the back!"

The passengers moved with increasing urgency, pushing past him and fighting through to the back of the train. A baby screamed. A woman cried. Somebody shouted a blatant refusal to step out between the cars.

Reed ignored them all and burst into the last car.

Lights flashed outside the windows—they were passing through Kensington Station. As the lights of the city glowed in ambers and reds, gleaming in muddled blurs through the windows, the prerecorded voice of the announcer kicked in overhead.

"The next station is Indian Creek Station. This is the end of the line."

Reed grabbed the handle into the driver's pod. It was locked. He drew the Glock from his belt and fired four rounds into the handle. Screams burst from the crowd behind him, and he kicked the door, breaking the latch, and then jerked it open.

Blood covered the floor. The driver lay stretched out in front of him with two bullet holes in her chest. Reed lunged over her, and then he saw Banks standing to his left, outside of the dirty windshield, with her face pressed against the glass. Her hands were bound by cuffs to the security latch at the top of the door.

Reed shoved past the driver's seat and pulled the first red lever he saw. Something snapped, and the train lurched and slowed a little, but it didn't stop. He jerked the lever again. This time it was limp, flopping in its channel like a broken arm.

One mile ahead, under a highway overpass and just beyond the offloading deck of the Indian Creek Station, red lights lit up the outline of the metal train stop.

The end of the line.

31

R eed fired twice into the window to the left of the door, then sent his fist crashing through the glass. Wind whistled through the interior of the car, carrying Banks's scream with it.

He pushed his arm through the hole and grabbed her by the arm.

"Banks! Come toward me!"

The wind tore the long blonde hair out of her face, and she looked up at him. "Chris?"

"Come toward me!" He pulled on her arm, but she shook her head.

"I can't move! I'll fall!"

"I'm going to cut the handcuff. I want you to move to your right so I can open the door!"

She shook her head again. "No, I can't—"

Reed didn't wait for her to finish. He jammed the pistol through the hole with his left arm and pointed it toward the chain of the handcuff. He fired once. The chain burst and Banks started to fall backward, but

Reed grabbed her by the arm and pulled her toward the left of the train.

"Hold on!"

She wrapped her hands around the rubber of the window frame. Shards of glass still stuck from the edges, and she cried out in pain as they sliced into her hand, but she didn't let go.

Reed jammed the Glock into the holster and shoved the handle on the emergency door. It popped, but the door was pinned closed by the force of oncoming wind. He pushed it forward, forcing it open far enough for him to slip through. He fought for purchase on the front of the car until his boot found the same narrow lip that he had used on the other end of the train.

Banks screamed over the roar of the wind. "Let me in!"

Reed shook his head.

"We're about to crash! We've got to jump!"

"Are you insane?"

Reed looked over his shoulder. Indian Creek Station was a hundred yards away, and less than four hundred yards farther, the train stop loomed up out of the dirt.

He didn't have time to argue. He wrapped his powerful right arm around Banks's torso and pulled her into him, twisting her around until they faced each other. He inched his way along the front of the car, clinging to the broken window frame with his left hand.

"Grab my chest rig and hold on!"

Her eyes were wild with panic, but she grabbed the

chest plate, planting her face against the rough fabric. The train station flashed past them on the right, and nothing but a wide-open ditch and trees stood to the left of the tracks. Reed let go of the window frame, wrapped both arms around Banks, and then launched himself away from the car.

As the train rocketed past, they flew through the air, spinning over the ditch. He clung to Banks like she was the only person left on Earth, holding her close with his arms wrapped around her back. An unearthly slamming and screeching sound exploded behind them, and then they landed.

Reed hit the dirt first, then tumbled over Banks as they crashed through the leaves and low underbrush. Dirt filled his mouth, and he lost his grip on her as his legs flew over his head and he continued rolling. His hips collided with the base of a tree, bringing his rampage through the undergrowth to a sudden stop.

The sky spun overhead. He twisted his neck and saw the train lying in a pile of mangled cars. All but the last two had flown off the rails and rolled into the ditch. The passengers were piled in the last car, and nobody moved.

Reed tried to roll to his knees, but the pain was too much. He could barely see, and his mouth filled with blood. Banks lay face up on the ground, still and silent, blood streaming from her temple.

"No . . ." Reed hissed. He rolled onto his stomach and crawled toward her. Every part of him burned with pain, but he put his palm against her throat and felt for a pulse. Nothing.

He clawed the phone out of his pocket and fumbled to unlock it before pressing the first contact.

A female voice answered almost immediately. "Where are you?"

"Indian Creek . . . Station. MARTA."

"Don't move. I'm coming."

Reed collapsed.

32

He heard the rustling of sheets first, then the faint sensation of something prodding his feet. His eyelids felt like they were weighted down by a ton of bricks.

Reed tried to open his mouth, but his tongue was dry. He coughed, then he felt a tube prodding between his lips. Cold water flowed over his tongue, wetting his throat, and he gulped it down. The stream continued for a few seconds longer before it was removed.

A grey ceiling filled his vision overhead, and he heard the faint whir of a fan, but he couldn't see it through his blurry vision.

"Can you hear me?" It was the familiar voice again.

"Kelly. I can hear you."

"Excellent. Take your time."

Reed couldn't remember anything. "Where was I?"

A soft laugh. "The usual. Lying in the middle of a cloud of dust and chaos."

That sounded right. His mind was fuzzy, but details began to return. "Banks."

He twisted his head and saw a short, brunette woman in her late twenties sitting on a stool next to him, her arms crossed as she stared back. Wavy hair was pushed behind her ears, and her brown eyes flashed.

"You mean the blonde girl?"

"Yes."

Kelly grunted. "She's alive. They had her in ICU at Grady, but I think they moved her to a regular room today."

Reed let out a sigh and slumped against the pillow. "Thanks, Kelly."

She snorted. "That's it? You don't want to know your situation?"

He attempted a shrug, but the movement sent searing pain across his chest. "I assume I'm alive."

"Yeah, you're alive. You don't deserve to be, but there's nothing new in all that. You've got fractured ribs, a seriously sprained ankle, a deep bullet graze on your left leg, severe lacerations over your back, a definite concussion—"

"How long?"

Kelly raised an eyebrow. "Until you and I can take a tumble between the sheets or until you can get back to blowing people away?"

Reed forced a smirk. "Is there a difference?"

Kelly stood up, retrieving a purse and shoveling personal effects into it. "You can go home tomorrow. I'll have you loaded up with some heavy-duty pills. You're beat up pretty hard, but nothing life-threatening. I stitched up your leg and put a brace on your ankle. Ideally, you should stay off your feet for a few days. But of course, you're not going to listen to me."

Reed tried to smile. "You're the best, Kel."

Kelly lingered next to the bed, the keys dangling from her fingers. She stared at him a long time, then slowly shook her head. "Dammit, Reed. This is the last time. I'm not patching you up anymore. I'm engaged now. I'm gonna settle down. Have a family. I can't have you barging into my life every two months needing illegal medical care."

Reed closed his eyes and nodded. "Don't worry. I won't call you again. I'll set you up with a sweet engagement present."

She smacked him with the keys, and when he opened his eyes, he saw that hers were rimmed with red. She leaned down and gave him a hug, then kissed him on the cheek.

"I would have married you if you weren't such a walking disaster."

She walked toward the door, her tennis shoes squeaking on the linoleum. The keys rattled against the lock, then she turned back.

"Let her go, Reed. Whoever she is. I saw the look in your eyes when you said her name. Take it from me . . . you break hearts a lot better than you break necks."

Reed stared at Kelly. Her deep brown eyes were sad and quiet, but there was peace in them. Kindness. It was a peace he hadn't seen there in a long time, as though her warning came from a place of quiet confidence, not bluster.

He closed his eyes and leaned back into the pillow. The door shut, and Kelly was gone. As silence filled the room, Reed tried not to think about her. He tried to push out the memories of the blonde girl with the ukulele—the smile on her face, her beautiful voice. The way her eyes flashed in the city lights.

But as his mind drifted into oblivion, those eyes were the last thing he saw.

33

Atlanta, Georgia

Grady Memorial Hospital sat in the heart of the city. It rose above the tangle of concrete structures and streets, towering in all of its old glory as one of Atlanta's keystone hospitals. Reed stood outside the main entrance and tilted his head back, staring up at the tall building. His neck hurt. Actually, his whole body ached, but Kelly's drugs were working all the magic he could hope for. They numbed enough of the pain so he could walk, and the rest would fade in time.

Reed looked toward the northeast. He couldn't see the west faces of 191 Peachtree or the Equitable Building, but he knew they were both laced with crime scene tape. The blown-out window on the forty-fifth floor of the 191 building was patched with thick plastic, pending a full replacement. The bleeding mannequin was gone, as were the ropes from the Equitable Building. The news stories Reed read earlier that morning postulated on every possible explanation for the bizarre events just days before, including drugged-up vagabonds, terrorists, and even a satirical article blaming it all on Batman.

The explanations for the derailed train were much more sinister, which was to be expected, considering the dead driver and all the mortified civilians on board. Several of the passengers sustained broken arms and concussions, but nobody died. Reed was thankful for that.

The investigations into the events around the towers and the train would turn against him. Cameras inside the trains would have captured his face. They wouldn't know who he was, and part of Oliver's detailed recruitment program involved washing Reed's fingerprints from national databases, so when the police found the abandoned submachine gun in the tunnel, they wouldn't be able to trace it back to him. But it was only a matter of time. Oliver would feed them what they needed to know, step back, and let the law do his dirty work for him.

Reed knew he should've been gone already. Everything about his training and the voice of survival in the back of his head commanded him to go. Even now, at the front entrance to Grady, Reed almost turned away. By midnight, he could be in another country. Within twenty-four hours, another continent. Far, far away from the claws of the FBI.

But he had to see her again. One last time.

He adjusted the shoulder holster under a new Panthers jacket, pulled the ball cap low over his ears, then stepped through the sliding glass doors. The busy main floor of the hospital hummed around him, and he pulled the jacket closer around his torso as he walked to the elevator. With the heel of his hand, he pressed the button to select the fifth floor, and then pulled a stick of gum from his pocket and jammed it between his teeth. The elevator rose slowly, and Reed chewed and tapped his foot with methodical nervousness, feeling suddenly closed in.

The doors opened, and he shuffled towards the nurses' station, waiting for them to acknowledge him.

"Can I help you?"

Reed glanced around the hospital hallways. The squeak of a wheelchair passed behind him. Computers beeped. A keyboard clicked.

"Sir?"

Reed clamped down on the gum, then without a word, shifted on his feet back toward the elevator.

"Chris?" The excited voice rang from behind, and Reed stopped. He almost walked forward again. Almost hit the elevator button.

But instead he turned, and there she was. Banks stood across the room wearing a loose T-shirt. Her left arm was held in a sling, both hands were bandaged, and on the outside of her sweatpants, she wore a brace around one knee. Her hair fell down behind her ears, and she wasn't wearing makeup.

The breath caught in his throat as he stared at her. Every noise he had obsessed over only moments before faded, carrying the stress and paranoia about being captured with them. She had never been more beautiful.

Banks broke into a big grin and limped toward him. Without hesitation, she wrapped him in a one-arm hug, pulling him closer toward her. "Chris! I couldn't find you."

Reed shifted, keeping his hands in his pockets. He could smell her hair and wanted so badly to sweep her off her feet. He could imagine her cheek pressed against his shoulder, her body cradled in his arms. His own person who cared for him and wanted him as much as he cared for and wanted her.

A home.

But Reed didn't move. He remained stiff and awkward. Unsure.

Banks smiled. "I'm glad you're okay."

For a moment, he couldn't do anything but stare, but he swallowed the gum and coughed. "I was, uh . . . at another hospital."

"Are you okay?" The concern in her voice was so sincere and innocent. She *did* care about him.

"Yeah, I'm great. Just a few bruises."

Banks reached up and touched his cheek, stroking it with the tips of her fingers, then she stood on her toes and kissed him softly. Sweetly.

Lost in the kiss, the world around him no longer mattered, and everything faded into perfect bliss.

Banks leaned back. "Thank you."

Those simple words knocked the wind right out of him. He wondered how the hell this girl could be so calm. She was strapped to the front of the train and sent hurtling toward her death before jumping from the moving car and rolling into battered unconsciousness. She was kidnapped, probably harassed, and mentally tormented. She almost certainly thought she would die.

Thank you?

Reed didn't know what to say. The knot in his stomach was like molten iron.

"Who are you, Chris? Why were you there?"

This was the question he dreaded. The one that kept him away from the hospital all morning, and probably should have kept him away altogether.

"I was at the station," he lied. "I saw the train pass. I just . . . did what I could."

The words stung him, and he wondered if she saw through the paper-thin sham.

Instead of pressing for specifics, Banks tilted her head toward the hallway.

"Come on. There's somebody I want you to meet."

Reed hesitated, but she grabbed his hand. They walked down the hall until she stopped at a closed door. Blocking the way was a Georgia State Police officer, glaring at him and cradling an AR-15 in his arms. Reed thought he was about to get frisked, so he tucked his left arm closer to his shoulder holster and started to turn back.

Banks pulled him forward. "It's fine, officer. He's with me."

The officer grunted and stepped to the side. Banks opened the door, and Reed ducked his head, slipping into the room. Another officer sat in the corner with a pistol strapped to his hip and a rifle leaning against the chair next to him. A tall woman dressed in a dark business suit stood next to the bed. She held a tablet and was busy tapping on the screen.

Lying in bed, bandaged up with tubes and wires strapped to his arm, was Senator Mitchell Holiday.

Reed relaxed his shoulders and allowed Banks to lead him toward the bed. The senator broke into a big smile when he saw Banks. She smiled back, and Reed forced himself to further relax his defensive stance.

"Uncle Mitch, I want you to meet someone." She turned toward Reed, and the smile she offered him was as warm and soft as the Caribbean sun. "This is Chris. He's the one who saved me."

Holiday's face was tired and sported a couple dark bruises. Reed knew where those bruises came from, and he also knew why the senator's chest was bandaged. He stared directly at Holiday and waited, bracing himself to run.

Holiday's face broke into a wide smile, and he offered his hand.

"Chris. Such a pleasure. I can't thank you enough for what you did. You're a hero, son."

Reed took Holiday's hand and offered a small smile. "It's an honor, Senator. I'm glad you're okay. I understand you've been through quite an ordeal."

Holiday laughed. "You could say that. Mostly I'm just dehydrated. Hence all this crap stuck in my arm. But nobody wants to talk about that. Tell me about yourself. My goddaughter thinks you hung the moon."

Reed hesitated, but Banks grabbed his hand and led

him to the single empty chair. She perched herself on the left arm, and Reed reluctantly sat down beside her.

"What do you do, son? You military? You've got the bearing."

Reed tried to smile. Holiday talked like a politician. "No, sir. I'm . . . a venture capitalist."

Holiday raised one eyebrow. "Really?"

Reed decided to run with the lie. "Yes. I work with small firms. Mostly out west. Invest and promote growth. It's all pretty boring."

Holiday tilted his head and squinted. "Have we met before? Something about you is familiar."

Reed forced a laugh and leaned back in the chair. "I get that a lot. A familiar face, I guess."

Holiday nodded slowly, then smiled again. "Well, I'm so drugged up, who knows? I'm a bit of a businessman myself, though. I'd love to hear more about your work. We should have lunch sometime."

Reed glanced at Banks sitting beside him. Her cheeks glowed, and her shoulders were relaxed into a casual slump. She looked happy, and he marveled at that. How could anyone experience the total terror she had been through and walk away so bright and alive? Maybe they gave her a sedative.

"Banks tells me you met at a bar," Holiday continued. "Hell of a second date."

Reed shifted on the chair and looked up at Banks. He wanted to scoop her up and kiss her, take her by the hand, and run like hell. Make her his. Love her and protect her and spend the rest of his life making her happy. They could escape this place and all the menacing dangers it held. Run so far into the sunset that nobody, not even his darkest enemies, could find them. Forget the west. They could leave the country, move to Asia or Africa, and build a simple home where he could be with her every day. Hold her and protect her and spend every morning staring into those eyes.

The daydream built in momentum, consuming him until his heart thumped. He stared at her so long, picturing every detail of her gorgeous face, that Banks tilted her head and squinted, dampening the innocence in her eyes.

In that moment, the daydream shattered. It fell around him like a glass statue exploding into a million pieces. Kelly's warning echoed in his mind, and he knew it then as clearly as he had ever known anything: he was a killer. This woman was an angel. As desperately as Reed longed for a home—a peaceful place to call his own—and as much as Banks felt like home, it wasn't fair. She was innocent and beautiful, a priceless artifact from an untarnished world, so far removed from his own that he didn't even speak the same language. His life was one of deceit and shadows and bloodshed—a violent, unpredictable, hostile world with deathtraps and menace at every corner. A harsh, cold place that was no habitat for love, and no home for happiness. He might escape that life, eventually, but he could never escape the reality of what it had done to him or who he had become.

That was a reality that this goddess from another life could never, ever be touched by. She deserved more.

Reed looked away.

"Actually, Senator, I have to be going. I've got some business in Europe. I just wanted to stop by and check on Banks."

Holiday frowned, and Reed wasn't sure if the senator was angry or just confused. Either way, he offered his hand again, and Reed stood up and shook it. Banks got up, and the soul-crushed look on her face was more than he could bear. He nodded at her and then pulled the hat down over his ears and walked toward the door. The guard let him out, and Reed accelerated toward the elevator.

He heard the door shut behind him, and another set of footsteps rang in the hallway.

"Wait!"

Reed stopped and felt the burn of tears sting his eyes. Everything in his body begged him to stop and turn around. To scoop her up. To hold her close and never, ever let go. He wanted that more than he wanted his next breath. He turned around, and she stared at him with red-rimmed eyes.

"That's it?" she mumbled. "You're just . . . leaving?"

The molten feeling in his stomach felt like a hurricane, but the feeling still wasn't strong enough to wash away the inescapable truth. He couldn't be hers, and she could never be his. He was at war now. A war that would be long and brutal and would get people hurt. Banks couldn't be one of those people. She had already suffered too much at the hands of Reed's dark underworld.

"Take care of yourself, Banks. You're an amazing woman."

Without another word, he turned and pushed through the doorway to the stairwell, leaving Banks standing in the hallway. The steps clicked under his feet, matching the tempo of his pounding heart.

As he shoved his way through the crowded waiting room and back onto the sidewalk, the cold breeze stung his face and chilled his cheeks. He looked up at the sky and felt the warmth of the sun on his face, remembering the touch of her lips on his and her amazing eyes shining with so much life and passion.

Nothing had ever felt so much like home.

Reed shoved his hands into his pockets, and without looking back, turned away from the city and walked to the terminal. The white MARTA bus was just pulling up as he arrived. Reed paid the fare and took a seat in the back, where he settled in and jammed his hands into his pockets.

He took one final glance at the hospital as the bus turned northeast and drove out of the city. He imagined Banks standing in a window, staring down at him, and waving goodbye. And he realized, just then, that he was leaving a part of him behind that he didn't know existed. All his life the world had taken things from him—his parents, his integrity, his freedom, his identity. He didn't think he had anything left to lose, and yet, in this moment, he realized just how much anyone could lose. The home that he longed for wasn't a building or an address on a quiet street. It was so much simpler than that—so much more internal.

He just wanted to belong.

Reed closed his eyes. He took a deep breath, and when he opened his eyes again, he forced out the memories, the hopes, the daydreams, and clenched his fingers around the arms of his chair.

He may not have a home, but that didn't mean he didn't have a place to go. Reed had a promise to fulfill— a promise to complete thirty kills. With twenty-nine down, Reed knew exactly who his next target would be.

He pictured the face and imagined the crosshairs settling over the base of the neck behind the balding head. He imagined the touch of steel beneath his trigger finger and the snap of the gunshot.

Twenty-nine kills. Oliver would be thirty.

Want to find out what happened in Iraq?

Read *Sandbox*, the Reed Montgomery prequel for FREE.

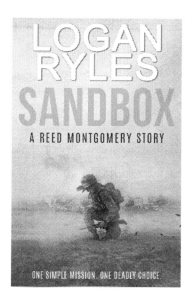

Visit <u>LoganRyles.com</u> to download your copy.

THE STORY CONTINUES WITH...

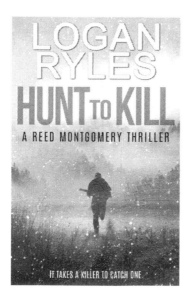

Turn the page to read the first chapter.

HUNT TO KILL

REED MONTGOMERY BOOK 2

November 24, 2014
United States Military Court
Washington, DC

"Reed Montgomery, on the charge of conduct unbecoming a United States Marine, you have been found *guilty*. On the charge of five counts of first-degree murder, you have been found *guilty*. You are hereby stripped of your rank and dishonorably discharged from the United States Armed Forces."

The judge paused over the conviction papers, his weary shoulders dropping a little but his tone remaining resolute.

"The murder of Private Jeanie O'Conner was a deplorable act. But I nevertheless find your deliberate execution of five US citizens to be a crime of the worst character, and I am unconvinced of any remorse on your part. I am therefore compelled to sentence you to death. Sergeant, take the guilty into custody!"

The gavel rang like a gunshot. The sharp *shrick* of the corporal patches being torn from Reed's sleeves filled his ears, screaming over the pounding of blood. Cold cuffs closed around his wrists, and the tall military policeman wearing sergeant's patches grabbed him by the arm and shoved him toward the door. Boots clicked on the tile, and the air was thick and hot, like the oppressive nights of Baghdad.

Private Rufus "Turk" Turkman, Reed's long-time brother-in-arms, stood next to the door. Reed met his gaze and mouthed a single word: "Goodbye."

"Next!" The stocky sergeant behind the desk bellowed at the line of white-clad prisoners without looking up. His face was pale and blotchy, betraying a life spent sitting behind that desk, away from the sun, and barking at convicts.

Reed shuffled forward, twisting his wrists against the tight cuffs. His footfalls rang against the blank block walls, leaving dark black scuffs on the dirty concrete. In the corner, a desk heater's electric coils glowed red in a futile attempt to provide warmth to the uninsulated space.

"Name," the sergeant demanded.

"Montgomery. Reed."

A pen scratched on yellow paper. The metal table squeaked under the pressure, and Reed swallowed back the knots in his stomach. He twisted his wrists again and tried to keep from shivering.

God, it's cold. The whole place can't be this cold.

"All right." The sergeant spoke without looking up. "Listen carefully, and don't speak until I'm finished. You are a prisoner of the United States Armed Forces. While renovations are completed at Fort Leavenworth, you will be housed at this facility. As such, you are our guest and will behave accordingly at all times. Is that clear?"

"Yes."

"Excellent. This institution is the property and function of the state of Colorado, and you can expect it to be operated according to our laws. Colorado does not automatically isolate death row inmates such as yourself. You will be confined in gen pop with other max security prisoners. This housing arrangement is a *privilege*, and can and will be revoked at any time should you become insubordinate. Do you understand?"

"I do."

"Good. You will abide by all daily functions, including lights out, waking hours, housekeeping duties, and any commands given to you by correctional officers. Any insurrection, insubordination, contraband, violence, or disruptive behavior will be swiftly and severely punished. Is that clear?"

"Yes."

The sergeant laid down the pen, and for the first time, he faced Reed. "You carry a death sentence. Men such as yourself often find themselves feeling desperate. Listen to me carefully when I tell you we do not tolerate desperate behavior. No matter who you are or where you came from, I promise you, you *do not* want to test us. This isn't a white-collar resort with a chain-link fence. We have the power to make your life absolute hell. Do you understand me?"

The heater hummed in the corner, providing the only variance to the silence. Those wide, bloodshot eyes didn't blink, and neither did Reed's. Seconds dripped by as though they were falling from a slow-leaking faucet.

"So, you're one of those." The sergeant nodded and tapped his pen against the table. "We'll see how long that lasts. Officer Yates! Show the convict to his cell."

An iron grip latched around Reed's arm, and he was propelled out of the room through a back door and into a long hallway. The CO's boots clicked amid the shuffle of the ankle chains, and with each step, Reed's chest constricted a little tighter. Dim lights shone down over him, barely illuminating the black dirt packed into the floor's cracks or the scratches in the paint along the walls. Dingy yellow ceiling panels hung overhead, completing the mood of the most utilitarian, unwelcoming place Reed could imagine.

"Move it, con." The correctional officer snapped and pushed harder. The chains caught on his ankles, and Reed stumbled around the corner. Two more halls, one flight of steps, and then a tall metal door with no window. Voices and footsteps rang out on the other side, pounding through a cavernous room beyond. Reed tripped over the threshold and fell to his knees, crashing against concrete. White pants flashing back and forth across the floor filled his vision.

A hundred yards ahead of him, standing in neat two-story rows, were dozens of small cells. Steel bars with open sliding doors guarded them, and a hundred white-clothed convicts wandered around the floor. Fluorescent light glowed from someplace far above, joined by a single bar-covered window at the top of the wall. The floor was as hard as the block hallways behind him, and there was no other way out. No doors. No color. No warmth. Only cold, brutal containment.

The CO grabbed him by the arm and hauled him to his feet. His fingers dug into Reed's arm, sending waves of pain shooting up to his shoulder. He fought to find his footing as he was shoved forward.

"Welcome to Rock Hollow Penitentiary, Number 4371."

"What's your name?"

Reed sat on the edge of the bed, his feet resting on the cell's chilled floor. He rubbed his bare wrists, massaging the bruises left by the cuffs. The thin white coverall suit he wore was incapable of blocking the bite of impending winter. Nothing could stop that scourge.

"Hey. You deaf?"

Reed looked up. A tall, skinny man with a shiny bald head and no hair on his pale face stood in the doorway to the cell, one hand resting on the wall, the other jammed in his pocket. His eyes were grey and hollow, like twin black holes frozen over.

"I'm Reed." The words left his lips as a dry monotone. He swallowed and tried to clear his throat.

The tall man nodded, still expressionless. "Is that right? Well, what the hell are you doing on my bed, Reed?"

Reed placed his hands on the thin blanket stretched over the cheap mattress. The stiff plastic sheathing crackled under his touch. He stood up and stepped away, offering a small shrug. "I'll take the top."

Reed placed his palms on the top bunk, preparing to lift himself onto the mattress, when cold fingers wrapped around his wrist, tightening into his skin.

The tall man leaned in close, his breath, reeking of garlic and cheap food, misting just inches from Reed's face. "That's my bed, too."

The comment felt distantly preposterous to Reed, as though he should laugh. But through the fog of disorientation, he couldn't make sense of it. He tilted his head and stepped back, gesturing toward the small cell. "Where the hell do I sleep?"

The man laughed, then jerked a thumb toward the stainless steel toilet mounted against the wall. "Sitting up. Like the bitch you are."

Reed stared at the toilet. The comments didn't register. Was this a joke? Was this man insane?

"Hey! What'd I tell you about coming in here? Get your skinny ass back into the hall!"

A snapping, high-pitched voice filled the cell, coming from behind the tall man. Reed started and stepped back as a short guy with dark hair barreled through the door. He wore the same white coveralls, but they fell low around his ankles and almost covered his hands. He couldn't have been more than five and a half feet tall, but his shoulders bulged, and even through the loose outfit, Reed could see the power of his muscled core.

The short man grabbed the tall one by the back of his coveralls and shoved him toward the door with another curse. "Go back to your hole, creep! I catch you slinking around here again, and you'll catch a shiv in the ribs. You hear me?"

The tall man cast one more sinister look toward Reed, then vanished down the hallway. The sound of barking voices from the crowd of convicts drowned out his footfalls. Reed leaned against the wall, feeling all the more disoriented.

The short man ran his fingers through dark curls, still glowering at the door. Then he shot a semi-interested glance at Reed. "You must be the fresh meat. Welcome to the pen." He extended his fist, then waited for Reed to bump it. His knuckles were hard with thick callouses built over them. He nodded at Reed once, then turned toward the bed and began to stretch the wrinkles out of the blanket. "I'm Stiller. You can call me *Still* if you want. I'm your celly. You want top or bottom?"

Reed placed his hand on the rail of the top bunk and ran his finger against the smooth surface. Flecks of ancient lead paint and grime rained onto the floor, and the stench of unwashed bodies and years of sweat filled his nostrils. The edge of the rail dug into his finger, and he dropped his hand back to his side.

I've slept on concrete that was more welcoming.

Stiller waited, then chuckled. "The fresh meat daze! Still can't believe it's real, huh? Well, take it from me, homie. It's real. Sooner you own it, the better your life will be. You take the bottom bunk. I won't sleep well with a dude your size hanging over me."

Stiller kicked off his shoes before hoisting himself onto the upper bunk. "You got a name or what?"

"Reed. Reed Montgomery."

"A pleasure, Reed. What'd you do?"

Reed folded his arms and leaned against the wall. The concrete bit into his shoulder blades, but he didn't move. He clenched his fists into his armpits and closed his eyes.

Stiller laughed again. "So, you're one of those. Whatever makes you feel better. Myself, I got busted dealing dope. I got a dime, still eight to go."

Reed pushed his hands into his pockets, searching for warmth to thaw his numb fingers.

"At least tell me how long you're in for," Stiller said.

Reed hesitated, then slumped over. It didn't really matter, he guessed. "Until they finish renovations at Leavenworth. I'll be there until . . . it's over."

Stiller frowned, tilting his head, and then an apparent realization dawned on him. He sighed. "Damn sorry to hear that, Reed. May you find favor with the appeals gods."

Reed shrugged and looked out into the hallway. "Who was he? The tall guy."

Stiller grunted. "They call him *Milk*. No idea what his real name is. Even the COs call him that."

"Is he dangerous?"

Stiller chuckled again. The sound was strangely comforting.

"Dude, you need to understand something. *Everyone* in here is dangerous. Milk isn't particularly burly, but he's shady and ruthless, and he's got a lot of friends. A lot of bitches, too—people who fear him and run his errands. My guess is, he was here to test the waters with you."

Reed stared into the hallway, rubbing his fingers together inside the pockets. They were still numb, but a hint of warmth built between the folds of the fabric.

"Did he try to push you around? Demean you?" Stiller said. Reed grunted, and Stiller leaned back into the pillow. "Yep. He's testing you. Better deal with it, Reed. It's not something you wanna leave hanging."

Reed kicked off his shoes and sat on the edge of the bed, looking at the blank, merciless floor between his feet. "I'm not here to fight. I just wanna—"

"Do your time and be left alone." Stiller finished the sentence with another snort. He rolled over on the bunk, and then his head appeared upside down next to Reed's. He had a handsome face with two days' worth of scruff on his cheeks. "Let me give you some advice, Reed. Best case scenario, you get off death row and spend the rest of your life inside a cell. Worst case scenario, you work through the appeals courts for the next ten years, and they still kill you. Either way, you're gonna be in prison for a hot minute. It's up to you how hot that minute is." Stiller slid off the bunk and shoved his feet back into the shoes, then shuffled through the open door.

Metal and shoes rattled outside the cell, and the grey walls around Reed blurred out of focus. Everything closed around him, drawing in toward his skull. Reed staggered to the sink and splashed water on his face, gasping for air as he clutched the edges of the basin. His reflection in the dirty mirror showed the white pallor of his cheeks and the panic in his eyes.

I can't stay here.

READY FOR MORE?

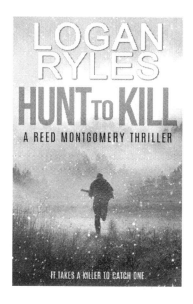

Visit LoganRyles.com for details.

ACKNOWLEDGMENTS

Overwatch was the journey of a thousand miles, and that journey began a long time ago when I first sat down and decided to write a book.

Twelve years and six books later, I have more people to thank for finally making it into print than I can fit on this page, but I would be remiss not to attempt an expression of gratitude for all the wonderful generosity that has helped me along the way. Here are a few mentions:

First, my loving wife Anna, who tirelessly supports me at every stage of my creative pursuits, listening to me ramble about my stories, sacrificing time together to allow me to work, and enduring round after round of editing with more enthusiasm than I usually feel myself. This book is as much her creation as mine, and I owe much more than just this story to her love and dedication.

My brother, 2Lt. Isaac King, United States Army, who has supported my dreams of being a writer since I was five years old, and continues to support them, read my books, and encourage me to keep going.

My parents, Tony and Karen, who have invested in and supported my creative pursuits since childhood and continue to love and support me as my work has evolved. Without their early investment in my writing interests, I never would have written this novel.

My other brothers, Adam, Noah, Micah, Samuel, Benjamin, and my baby sister Hannah, who love and support me and have always loved my stories.

My good friend, mentor, and fellow novelist, Cap Daniels, whose advice, companionship, and support has opened countless doors and enabled me to pursue a career in publishing. My work is unspeakably better due to his guidance and encouragement.

My incredible editor, Sarah Flores of Write Down the Line LLC, whose endless patience and relentless dedication to her craft have made *Overwatch* readable. I cannot overstate how greatly her work, partnership, advice, and guidance have impacted both this work and my writing in general.

My adopted sister, Hannah Malone, who has supported, encouraged, and assisted in my writing for as long as we have been companions in crime. She has listened to me ramble on about my ideas over many an Angry Orchard, and she has provided the sort of snarky feedback that only a sister could give.

My brother-in-law, Capt. Joel Pendleton, Southern Airways Express. Joel's hard-driving, tireless dedication to pursuing his dreams of becoming an airline pilot inspired me to keep fighting for my own dreams, and his friendship and support of my writing have further fueled the fire.

My entire advance reader team, including Ike, Joel, Hannah, Alex Flanders, and Michael and Katie Farrar.

This team read the advance copy of *Overwatch*, providing critical last-minute feedback and support.

I also owe thanks to the city of Atlanta, which has housed me on many a lonely night when I needed to clear my mind and try to make sense out of this thing we call life. The people of Atlanta are some of the finest I've ever met, and I will always know the Empire City of the South as my soul city. It was a tremendous honor to write a story set on those old streets, and I hope I brought to life the charm of Atlanta in these pages.

ABOUT THE AUTHOR

Logan Ryles was born in small town USA and knew from an early age he wanted to be a writer. After working as a pizza delivery driver, sawmill operator, and banker, he finally embraced the dream and has been writing ever since. With a passion for action-packed and mystery-  laced stories, Logan's work has ranged from global-scale political thrillers to small town vigilante hero fiction.

Beyond writing, Logan enjoys saltwater fishing, road trips, sports, and fast cars. He lives with his wife and three fun-loving dogs in Alabama.

Visit his website at www.LoganRyles.com

f

ALSO BY LOGAN RYLES

The Reed Montgomery Series

The Prosecution Force Series

The Wolfgang Pierce Series

LoganRyles.com)

The Mason Sharpe Series

LOGANRYLES

LoganRyles.com

Made in the USA
Las Vegas, NV
24 February 2023

68060519R00171